BBC

DOCTOR WHO

THE GOOD DOCTOR

DOCTOR WHO

THE GOOD DOCTOR

JUNO DAWSON

3 5 7 9 10 8 6 4

BBC Books, an imprint of Ebury Publishing
20 Vauxhall Bridge Road,
London SW1V 2SA

BBC Books is part of the Penguin Random House group of companies whose
addresses can be found at global.penguinrandomhouse.com

Penguin
Random House
UK

Copyright © Juno Dawson 2018

Juno Dawson has asserted her right to be identified as the author of this Work in
accordance with the Copyright, Designs and Patents Act 1988

Doctor Who is a BBC Wales production.
Executive producer: Chris Chibnall, Matt Strevens and Sam Hoyle

First published by BBC Books in 2018

www.penguin.co.uk

A CIP catalogue record for this book is available from the British Library

ISBN 978 1 785 94384 3

Typeset in 11/14.3 pt Albertina MT Std
by Integra Software Services Pvt. Ltd, Pondicherry

Publishing Director: Albert DePetrillo
Project Editor: Steve Cole
Cover Design: Lee Binding/Tealady Design
Production: Sian Pratley

Printed and bound in Great Britain by Clays Ltd, Elcograf S.p.A.

Penguin Random House is committed to a sustainable future for
our business, our readers and our planet. This book is made
from Forest Stewardship Council® certified paper.

MIX
Paper from
responsible sources
FSC
www.fsc.org FSC® C018179

For Stuart, who told me all this was possible

Chapter 1

On the tank's monitor, General Orryx surveyed the ruins with keen yellow eyes. Kanda was once a proud, beautiful city. Now it was little more than rubble; only the charred skeletons of homes, temples and shops still stood.

By dawn the war would be over, and the loba would reclaim their world. "Lobos for loba," she often told her troops.

Kanda was the last stronghold of the rebels and Orryx had them surrounded. The tank bumped and shuddered as it ploughed over the debris. Hers was one of a fleet, all closing in on the city. For the human scum, there would be no escape.

'General Orryx,' said Captain Brun. 'Incoming. From above.'

Orryx checked her radar and, sure enough, a small flying object – possibly a drone of some sort – approached. 'What is that thing? Intercept it. Blast it out of the sky.' There was only room for two personnel in the tank, but they were flanked by hundreds of foot soldiers, ready to storm what was left of Kanda Plaza on her command.

'STOP!' The voice boomed from every speaker in the tank.

Orryx covered her ears and Brun yanked the headphones off his head. The tank stopped rolling, its engines dead. The few lanterns that still worked on the street flickered and went out. Even her scanners dimmed until the aux batteries kicked in.

'Who is that? Where is it coming from?' Orryx snarled, her eyes almost glowing in the gloom of the tank. 'Why did you stop?'

'I didn't, General! The controls are frozen. It won't move.'

'Where are the floodlights? Get me visual!' All she could assume was that the humans had somehow got their furless paws on alien technology. 'And destroy that drone! Now!'

'Weapons offline.'

Orryx's heart pounded. This wasn't possible. The rebels didn't have the means to ...

'IT'S ME. PLEASE. CEASEFIRE.'

Orryx recognised that voice very well.

'General?' Brun said quietly. 'It sounds like ...'

'Stop the assault. Now! Halt!' She spoke into the comms system. 'Fleet. Halt and ceasefire. That's an order. Over.'

The tank had enough power for her to use the visualiser. Orryx scanned the district. In the east, the suns were starting to rise, the sky almost violet-purple. With the tanks and bikes now still, the dust started to settle on Kanda Plaza. In the sky, a single light shone from a spherical drone. It hovered like it was waiting for her to make a move.

'What is that device?' Orryx growled.

'Negative, general. The scanner doesn't recognise the technology as human.'

'Is it a weapon?'

'I … I don't know, General.'

'MOTHER.' His voice once more blasted all around them. 'PLEASE. CAN WE TALK?'

There was a sudden flurry of movement on the deserted street. A drain cover popped open, rolled across the street and came to a stop with a clang. 'Hold fire!' Orryx commanded, trying to keep panic out of her voice. 'But train your guns on that storm drain.'

'Someone's coming out,' Brun told her.

A makeshift white flag emerged from the sewer. It appeared to be an article of clothing – a cotton shirt with the words FRANKIE SAYS RELAX in black, human script – attached to a bamboo cane.

'They're surrendering,' Brun whispered. 'We won.'

'Wait here. Unseal the hatch.'

'But General, they may have gas bombs or—'

'Do it!'

With a hiss, the hatch unlocked. Orryx twisted the handle and swung the door open. The air was gritty and dusty, tinged with acrid smoke and gunpowder. She pulled her scarf over her snout and mouth. From the drain, she saw Avi emerge, holding his flag. It took everything she had not to cry out and run to him.

She'd long since thought him dead.

There he was. *Alive.* As Avi crawled out into the rubble, he was followed by a human woman. She had yellow head fur and wore a long grey coat. She didn't look like a soldier at all; her trousers finished halfway up her legs for one thing. She too stumbled onto the plaza, her arms aloft in surrender. Behind her came an elderly human male and a face she recognised well: Alex Blaine, the resistance leader.

Faintly, she heard snipers ready their weapons. Her soldiers had them entirely covered on all sides.

'I said hold your fire or I will have your pelts!' she yelled. She would not risk her only son, not now that she had this second chance. *How?* How was this possible?

Orryx slid over the front of the tank and dropped down in the debris. She established that Blaine didn't appear to be holding a gun, but that meant nothing. He'd killed many, many loba in his time.

'Mother …' Avi began.

Orryx said nothing because she didn't trust herself not to cry and that would be unforgiveable in front of her troops. Her cub was fully grown now, taller than her. They were still unmistakably mother and cub, however: same eyes, same thick, shaggy chestnut fur.

'Mother … I …'

Suddenly, the human woman interrupted him, stepping between them. Up close, she was slight, impish. 'I'm sorry, but would you look at the state of this?' She twirled around, waving her arms at the ruins. 'Look at all this mess!'

As she spun closer, Orryx drew her gun. 'Stay where you are! Freeze!'

'But look at all this mess!' the woman said again, her eyes wide. Orryx wondered if maybe she was intoxicated.

'I won't warn you again …'

'Look at it.'

This time it was a demand. The human woman, somehow, was now almost nose to nose with her.

'What do you mean?'

'Just what I said. Look at the mess.'

She snorted. For the first time, Orryx looked at her feet. Scattered around her gleaming boots was all sorts of junk from the old marketplace.

The woman with yellow fur squatted down for a split second and bounced back up holding a chipped mug. 'Look.'

Orryx sighed. She didn't have time for this. 'It's a cup.'

'It's a *blue* cup.'

'I see that.'

'Probably belonged to someone, don't you think?' She pointed at the ruins. 'From one of those homes, I should think. I wonder if it was someone's *favourite* mug. I wonder if every morning, without fail, they'd wake up and make a lovely cup of tea in their favourite blue mug. I can't start the day without a cup of tea in my favourite mug, can you?'

'*What?*'

'I like Yorkshire Tea the best. What about you?'

Far away, on the other side of Kanda City, Yaz and Ryan crouched in the dark radio tower. It reeked of damp. Water ran down the black walls and wind howled through the corridors. This high up, it felt like the tower was swaying back and forth in the gusts.

Trying to ignore seasickness, Yaz could hardly believe Edwards had got this wreck to work. The young soldier looked out of the broken window with his binoculars. He can't have been more than fourteen years old, Yaz thought to herself. The torn camouflage he wore drowned him. 'It's transmitting,' he said. 'All over Lobos. Everyone can hear it.'

'Let me see,' Yaz said, tugging on Ryan's arm. 'Stop hogging it.'

The feed from the drone was – somehow – being picked up by Ryan's phone. 'It's broadcasting on every available frequency. Audio, visual … everything,' Ryan said. The Doctor had found the drone in the TARDIS storeroom and instructed Edwards to patch it into the old radio network. But, according to Edwards, this radio tower hadn't been used for years. The remaining equipment was rusty junk, but Edwards had managed to patch it up sufficiently to receive and transmit the signal.

'Fine!' Yaz said, 'But let me see.'

'Magic word?'

Yaz tutted. 'Please?'

He tilted his screen in her direction. She saw what the drone saw. It showed the Doctor, Graham, Avi and Blaine talking to someone she guessed was this Orryx she'd heard so much about.

Yaz frowned at Ryan. 'What's she doing with that mug, though?'

The yellow-haired one kicked through the rubble. Her hand shot out like a dart and this time seized a photo frame. 'I've always had a soft spot for a photo frame,' she said. 'Especially after the twentieth century when everything went digital because, to print out a photo and stick it in a frame, you really, really had to care about who was in that picture, right?'

She rubbed the shattered glass with her cuff.

'I wonder who they were. I mean, if this is half buried, they're dead, right?' She tossed the photo at Orryx's feet. 'Loba family, by the way, if it matters. Maybe it doesn't; maybe that's the picture that came with the frame.'

'Who are you? Explain yourself,' Orryx demanded.

'Mother, listen to her,' urged Avi.

'I've seen far too many wars,' the woman said, still pacing in the dirt, scuffing up dust. 'And if there's one thing I know to be absolutely, universally true it's this: if you stop and look in the rubble for about sixty seconds, you'll find … this!'

Almost out of thin air, the woman produced a filthy stuffed animal.

'A teddy bear with one eye.'

'Drop it!' Orryx said. It was a reflex and she felt ridiculous at once.

'It's harmless!' The woman now shouted, her smile, her jovial manner, all gone. 'Just like its owner was!'

She stepped up to Orryx, pushing her gun aside.

'That thing won't work. My little drone thingamajig up there is creating an electromagnetic wave that's disabling all your apparatus within a one-mile radius, I'm afraid. I wanted to talk, and you can't talk with a gun in your hand because the gun's doing all the talking.'

Orryx growled, baring her teeth. 'I could kill you with my bare hands, human.'

'What for? And I'm not human.'

'For ...' Orryx found she had no answer.

'I've only been here a few hours so, I wonder, if you could explain what all this is about? What are you fighting for? You'd be surprised how many soldiers forget.'

Orryx fought an urge to plunge her fangs into this human's scrawny neck, the way her ancient ancestors would have done. 'The humans ...'

'The humans what?'

'The humans stole our land.'

Blaine took a step forward. 'That's a lie! We were settled here legally and fairly ...'

'Let's allow the general to answer, shall we, Mr Blaine? You've had your turn!' The woman turned back to Orryx, fixing her with a hard stare. 'He's like a broken record that one. Tell me what the humans did, General Orryx. I'm listening.'

'Well.' Orryx threw her arms up, exasperated. 'The terms of the colonisation were agreed two generations ago. A thousand humans were allowed to settle. But they've grown, bred, expanded.'

'And?'

'And what?'

'And what's wrong with that?'

Orryx couldn't find the words. 'This ... this is our planet!' She regretted the words as soon as she said them. She sounded like Avi when he was a cub, refusing to share his toys with his cousins.

The human woman dared to smile a sly smile. 'Was there enough to go around? Enough food? Enough medicine? Enough shelter? Enough *kindness*?'

Orryx said nothing. She turned away.

'Tell me, General Orryx, tell me, Captain Blaine: is there any good reason on this planet why all these people had to die?' The woman crouched again and picked up a red plastic boot, a boot that would only fit a small child, from the wreckage. She waved it at both Orryx and Blaine in turn. 'Well? I'm waiting!'

Neither leader replied.

'No one ever wins at war. Not really.' The woman looked down at all the mess with such sadness in her eyes, Orryx could hardly bear to watch.

Avi came to his mother's side. 'Mother. This has to stop.'

'I thought you were dead,' Orryx whispered.

'Obviously not. Can you remember Cathie? From school?' A human girl with curly black hair and dark skin crawled out of the sewer. Orryx dimly remembered her face from when the schools had still been mixed before the laws changed. 'We're married now.'

It was like a punch in her gut, but before she had time to react there was a further surprise. As Cathie drew herself upright, Orryx saw she was carrying a litter. No, humans usually only birth a sole infant. In this case though, with one loba parent, who knew? This was unprecedented. 'Avi …? How can this be?'

'That's why I left you, Mother. I thought you would kill my wife, my child.'

'No!' Orryx said. 'I … Is that what you think of me?'

The one with yellow fur spoke again. 'People of Lobos!' she said to the sky, her arms wide. 'Thanks to my very clever friends Ryan and Yasmin, I know you're all hearing this. Every last one of you, loba and human. Now listen up because I am so bored, so sick to my very back teeth, of saying this. You've got a choice. Peace or war? Life or death? Harmony or hate? I've never understood why that even needs discussion, it's so flippin' obvious!'

'She don't half have a way with words, don't she?' The older human male with grey fur finally spoke.

'A lot of people have died in this war. And you and you …' the woman pointed at Orryx and Blaine, 'have the power to say "stop".'

Orryx watched as the girl, Cathie, joined Avi and took his paw in her hand.

'Call it a day, yeah?' the grey-furred one said.

Now the woman spoke softly, just to her. 'There is another way,' she said. 'Just take it.'

From the radio tower, Ryan and Yaz watched the scene play out on Ryan's phone. 'What's happening?' Ryan said. 'Why can't we hear 'em?'

'Um, because you won't stop talking over them?' Yaz said with a smile. 'I don't know.'

On the tiny screen, they saw Avi fall into his mother's arms and General Orryx held him tight. The general buried her face in her son's shoulder.

'She did it!' Ryan exclaimed. 'The Doctor actually did it! I don't believe it!'

'I do,' Yaz grinned. 'Man, she's good.'

There was a strong gust of wind and the entire structure leaned to the left. 'Whoa!' Ryan toppled into Yaz and they both slid across the floor towards the edge.

'Is this safe?' Yaz cried.

'C'mon,' said Edwards. 'We need to get out of this tower before the whole thing collapses.'

Well, that answered her question. Yaz sprung up and Ryan dashed after her. 'Wait for me!' He didn't fancy the stairs without having someone to grab hold of if he fell. He didn't like stairs at the best of times.

'I've got you,' Yaz muttered as she started the descent.

In their haste, neither of them noticed Ryan's phone underneath the sound desk, where he'd dropped it.

Chapter 2

The big sun and the little sun were starting to sink into the sea. It was a beautiful sunset. The TARDIS stood outside a taverna in what the locals called New Town. This was loba territory, on the other side of Kanda City to where the squalid human colony camps were. The fists of civil war hadn't pummelled this part of town half so badly. The difference from the twee little fishing town and the shacks where the humans lived was stark and left a bad taste in Graham's mouth, even as he finished his third glass of syrupy violetta wine.

While the Doctor was thrashing out the peace agreement, Graham, Ryan and Yaz enjoyed a platter of food and wine on the front terrace: salty meats and fish, fresh warm bread and a strange purple fruit that tasted like both limes and olives at the same time. It had been a long day, and there was still much to do, but at least Blaine and Orryx were talking without weapons in their hands. Graham felt that was a step in the right direction.

It was time for them to go. It was almost time for *Pointless*. Whatever the Doctor said about time travel, in

Graham's world, five-fifteen was *Pointless*, six sharp was dinner, and that wasn't going anywhere. That's how it was when Grace was alive and keeping their little routines alive felt only correct.

'It's beautiful, isn't it?' Yaz said, her feet up on the chair.

'Yeah. I hope it stays that way.'

'It will,' Yaz said. 'We fixed it.'

The doors swung outwards and everyone spilled out of the taverna, the Doctor leading the way.

'All done?' Graham asked.

Cathie gave him a big hug. 'Yes. And thank you, Graham. For everything.'

'Oh, I ain't done nothing.'

Her hands rested on her bump. 'You did! What you said about you and your wife being different species ...'

'I didn't say that, love! I said different *races*! Big difference!'

'Well it meant a lot.'

Graham smiled and returned her hug. 'You're welcome.'

The Doctor took Blaine's hand and placed it in Orryx's paw. 'You two are ... iconic!' she said, beaming at them. 'Do you know how many people died today? Zero! And that's all because of you. Brilliant!'

'Thank you, Doctor,' Orryx said.

'Keep it up. It's all up to you now. Let your names burn bright from the pages of the history books!'

Avi nervously stepped forwards, a clunky camera in his hands. 'Um ... may I?'

'Sure!' Yaz said.

The Doctor made a sort of humming noise, but allowed herself to perch on the edge of the group next to Cathie.

Graham stood in the middle between Orryx and Blaine, feeling very proud of everyone. 'Smile!' Avi said and the camera flashed.

Ryan and Yaz finished saying their goodbyes to Avi, Cathie and Edwards. The founders of a new Lobos.

'Come on you lot. The people of Lobos have a lot of work to do,' the Doctor said. 'And I think it's time we left them to it.'

'Good luck!' Yaz said, stepping into the TARDIS.

Ryan followed her in. 'See yer!'

'You look after each other, yeah? We've got a saying where we come from – dogs are man's best friends!' Graham laughed, pleased with his little joke. Planet of dog people! He'd been waiting to say it for almost two days.

'One, two, three,' the Doctor counted. Graham hovered at her side. 'Right! That's all of them. Off we go again.'

Blaine frowned. 'You all fit in there? How? It's a box.'

She smiled and gave a wink. 'Tell people it's a *magic* box. Always goes down well.'

'But Doctor,' Orryx said. 'What if we need your help? Things are so fragile. What if …?'

The Doctor held up a finger. 'Never mind "what ifs". The future is yours, make it work. If I've got to come back, there'll be bother. Now … behave yourselves!'

And with a final, manic, grin, the Doctor ducked inside her blue box. The door slammed shut and a second or two later, a wheezing-groaning noise filled the twilight air. The box faded from view.

Orryx looked to Blaine. 'Who *was* she?'

'I have no idea. A stranger and her friends. Come to save us all.'

Ryan loved to watch the Doctor dance with the TARDIS. That was what it was. Some days it was a jive, the Doctor jumping and prodding at the console, and some days it was more like a waltz; slow and deliberate. Today it was perhaps a flamenco type thing with added arm flourishes.

'Well hopefully that settles your argument,' the Doctor said as the TARDIS dematerialised. The vortex beyond the edges of the console room started to swirl and shift as they flew through space and time.

Yaz frowned. 'What? Ryan said dogs were cleverer than humans.'

The Doctor's eyes widened. 'Yeah. And I think I ably demonstrated that they're just as clever as each other. End of discussion.'

'She's got you there.' Ryan gave Yaz a nudge.

'OK, I owe you a fiver, whatever.'

Graham shook his head wearily, pulling off his shoes and giving his left foot a rub. 'This life you lead, Doctor. Absolutely mad. Barking mad.' A broad grin broke out on his face. '*Barking.* Geddit?'

The Doctor smiled, pulling a lever on the console. 'Ooh, you're wasted on us, Graham. You should be on the stage. Interesting story actually. Remember Laika? That poor doggo the Russians blasted into space? It's her DNA the loba ultimately evolved from.'

Yaz's jaw dropped. 'What? No way?'

The Doctor's eyebrows flashed up.

'As if! You're having us on? There's no way …?'

'Isn't there?'

The Doctor gave Ryan a sly smile, but he had no idea if she was kidding or not. You never could tell with her. He wondered what time it was on Earth. Somehow, wherever the TARDIS went, his phone maintained Sheffield time. Although he'd picked at the food in the taverna while Orryx and Blaine drew up the peace plan, right now he was starving. He patted his hoodie pockets and then his jeans but couldn't feel the familiar rectangle shape.

His heart sank.

It was the horrible feeling that you get when you're standing at a supermarket self-checkout and realise your wallet's at home. 'Oh, man.'

'What?' Yaz asked.

'Have you got my phone?'

'Why would I have your phone?' Her eyes widened. At the same time, they both realised where he'd had it last. 'Oh, Ryan, you didn't?'

Ryan did a quick loop of the console to make sure he hadn't put it anywhere, but it was nowhere to be seen.

'What's wrong?' the Doctor asked.

'He's lost his phone,' said Yaz. '*Again*.'

'Oh Ryan! Mate!' Graham sighed. 'You only got that last week.'

'I know! I know!' He was absolutely terrible with phones. He often wondered if he was cursed. He remembered his nan had once lent him some money to get a new one when he'd dropped the last one in the bath while taking a … well, the less said about that the better. 'Doctor, we've gotta go back. I can't afford another one.'

The Doctor didn't look thrilled at the prospect. Ryan had her down as someone who preferred forward momentum.

'Come on, please. It's brand new. Still has that little bit of plastic on the screen and everything. Please, please, please …?'

'Oh all right!' She ran a hand through her mop of hair. 'Do you know exactly where you left it?'

'Yep! In the radio control room.'

The Doctor considered this. 'Right. That structure wasn't stable. I'll materialise at the foot of the tower and we'll fetch it. In and out, understood?'

'Got you.'

A slight frown furrowed her brow. 'The loba and humans have a lot to sort out, and I'm not meant to "interfere", whatever that means. To be honest, I was never a hundred per cent clear on that bit.' The Doctor pulled her lever in the opposite direction and checked something on the monitor.

Graham raised a hand tentatively. 'Boss, we'll still be back in time for *Pointless*, right?'

The Doctor smiled as the TARDIS landed, the column grinding to a halt. 'Yasmin. You do the time travel explanation for Graham, yeah? We'll be back in five.' She took Ryan by the hand. 'Come on, you, let's make this a ninja-like return visit.'

The Doctor and Ryan crossed from the TARDIS into the night air. Ryan always found it so odd, that split second when he passed from the ship to wherever it had landed. It was like stepping out of a bubble without popping it.

But why was it night? It was pitch dark. When they'd left it had been a summery twilight.

'That's odd,' the Doctor said. 'We must have jumped forwards a few hours.'

'Or back?'

'I hope not, I don't fancy crossing paths with ourselves last night. Paradoxes are never fun.'

The Doctor surveyed the area. The TARDIS seemed to have materialised in one of the cobbled plazas of New Town. Lobos reminded Ryan of a messy holiday to Crete he'd once been on with his mates – the climate, the rocky hillsides rolling down to the sea. From what little he remembered of it, there were lemon groves everywhere and Lobos was similarly dotted with trees bearing the strangest purple fruit he'd ever seen. The bushes and vines chirped with what he hoped were crickets. He didn't take stuff like that for granted any more.

'This isn't the radio tower,' he said.

'I know.' The Doctor stroked the side of the TARDIS and gave it a pat. 'No one's perfect, Ryan. It's just on the other side of the hills, isn't it?'

'Yeah.'

'Off we go, then!'

'Do you want me to Google map it?'

The Doctor looked at him sympathetically as she started charging across the square towards the steep, winding road that led up the hillside out of Old Town. 'Ryan, Ryan, Ryan. One: my sense of direction is second only to my sense of righteous indignation, and two: the reason we're here is that you've lost your phone …'

'Oh. Yeah. Good point.'

Even though he towered over her, Ryan always struggled to keep up with the Doctor when she was on a mission – nothing to do with his dyspraxia and everything to do with her limitless energy.

Suddenly, the Doctor stopped dead in her tracks and Ryan crashed into her back. 'Oof! Sorry!'

'No,' the Doctor said. 'No, that was my fault.' She seemed to be staring up at the sky – the three moons all matching crescents of different sizes.

'What? What's up?'

She looked pale. 'Ryan. Do you notice anything a little bit different?'

He looked around, but everything looked pretty much the same in New Town. 'Nope.'

The Doctor rolled her eyes and took hold of his shoulders to steer him in the right direction. 'There!'

'Oh man.'

'Yep.' The Doctor's keen eyes cut through the night. 'Where did *that* come from?'

On the horizon, looming over the entire town was a vast tower. It was almost the same shape as a block of flats, but, even in the gloom, Ryan could see it was painted dark blue. There were huge rectangular windows at the top of the structure.

'Remind you of anything, Ryan?'

It was unmistakeable.

It was meant to be the TARDIS.

Chapter 3

Ryan gawped up at the structure. 'Is ... is that supposed to be ...?'

'Oh I think it just might be.' The Doctor paused for a moment. She hopped from foot to foot. Ryan knew this dance too. It was the *do we run away from this or towards it* dance. And he knew exactly which she'd choose. 'Come on, let's take a little look. There's only two things I don't believe in, and one's coincidence.'

She started once more up the hill, even faster than before.

'And what's the other?'

'Goblins. Actually never say never. OK, there's *one* thing I don't believe in.'

Soon Ryan was panting, taking huge strides just to keep up with her. 'Shouldn't we go back and tell the others?'

'Nah, they're perfectly safe down there. This'll only take a minute or two. I mean, it's a great whopping building that looks exactly like the TARDIS, I can't ignore it, but I don't especially need anyone to know we've been back.

They'll only invite us in for tea and lemon drizzle cake and we've got places to be. My hypothesis is we've jumped forward in time.'

'How far?'

'That's the correct question. Long enough to build that in any case. I am guessing it's a peace monument. Ryan! Look at that! We made history earlier! I *love* it when that happens! Let's have a quick look, feel lovely and glowy inside, and then get your phone.'

Ryan stopped, hands on hips. The night air was balmy, airless. He peeled off his hoodie. 'As if my phone is still gonna be there! It's fifty years in the past or something!'

'Oh. Good point. I suppose we can slip back in time easily enough afterwards. Come on, slowpoke! I'm two thousand years older than you and I'm not out of breath!'

Yaz lay flat on her back on the floor of the TARDIS.

'... I don't mind the Daily Catch,' Graham went on. 'That's the one on Palmer Road. But the batter's always a bit soggy, y'know what I mean? The Codfather just gets it the exact right level of crispy ... and they do scraps.'

Yaz sprung up. 'Where *are* they?' she said, exasperated. She couldn't take another second of takeaway chat. She checked some of the read-outs on the TARDIS console. She gave the dial a quick tap and the time sensors oscillated backwards. Now that was weird. Had they travelled in time? Was that supposed to happen? She was still very much learning how the TARDIS worked.

She'd learned on her very first day of training that a police officer should always trust her gut, and now that sixth sense was telling her something was pretty seriously up. Her intuition hadn't let her down yet. 'I'm gonna go look for them.' She set off for the doors.

Graham winced. 'Really? Not again …'

'What's that supposed to mean?'

He gave her a highly sceptical look. 'We all split up and look for clues like in *Scooby-Doo* and it don't ever end well …'

Yaz grinned. Valid point. 'I'll just make sure everything's cool. Wait here if you want.'

Graham grabbed his jacket once more. 'Not on your nelly. We'll stick together, thank you very much.'

'Thought so!' Yaz led the way out of the TARDIS and stepped back onto Lobos. It was a humid night, crickets and cicadas chirruping away like a little mariachi band. She didn't recognise the square; it was some sort of grove in the middle of some shops and stalls. At this time of night it was deserted, and the air smelled of the sweet purple ousfruits she'd sampled earlier in the taverna. 'Doctor? Ryan?' she stage whispered.

'What are we all the way down here for? Other side of town, ain't it?' Graham said, taking his coat and scarf off again and throwing them back through the TARDIS doors. 'Why didn't she just park outside the tower thing?'

Again, Yaz's intuition told her something had gone wrong, something more than just the TARDIS being less reliable than the 32A bus. She *knew* that the Doctor had told her to stay put, but if she and Ryan were in trouble, who else was gonna help them? And if they weren't in trouble, it was just an evening stroll. She vaguely remembered that the dilapidated radio tower was on the other side of the hill and inland. In any case, it was such an eyesore, it wouldn't be hard to find them. 'Let's head uphill,' she told Graham.

She'd also learned at police academy that half the trick is in *appearing* confident even when you aren't, so she set off with a lot more agency than she felt.

As soon as she turned the corner of the square, she pushed Graham back behind a bush. 'Oi!' he cried, but Yaz was more concerned by the drone that sped towards her.

'Get down and stay down!' she hissed. She held up her hand against its searchlight. From what she could tell it was very similar to the Urbankan drone she and Ryan had fetched from the TARDIS earlier to jam the radio signal, but this one was bigger and covered in vicious-looking, rusty spikes.

'Seriously, Graham. Stay back!' She spoke without mouthing her lips.

'HALT,' the drone said in a flat, robotic voice. Oh. Not only did it *look* different, it had learned to talk. 'IDENTIFY.'

Yaz held her hands up, backing towards the TARDIS inch-by-inch. 'I … I'm Yaz. Yasmin Khan. I'm unarmed. I mean no harm.' She saw Graham edging out of the bushes to help her and gave him a very subtle shake of her head. If she couldn't talk her way out of this, he was her only hope. Graham looked torn, but did as he was told.

A second little light flickered over her entire body. 'HUMAN FEMALE.'

'Yes. That's right.'

Yaz continued to reverse. 'I'm not doing anything wrong. I'll just be on my way ...'

'HALT. BOOK OF RULES CHAPTER THREE VERSE TWO: WOMANKIND IS FORBIDDEN FROM LEAVING THE HEARTH AND HOME AFTER DARK LEST SHE IS ATTENDED BY HER HUSBAND OR FATHER.'

Oh. Was this thing for real? 'What?'

'BOOK OF RULES CHAPTER THREE VERSE TWO: WOMANKIND IS FORBIDDEN FROM LEAVING THE HEARTH AND HOME AFTER DARK LEST SHE IS ATTENDED BY HER HUSBAND OR FATHER.'

'Yeah, I heard you.' The TARDIS must have somehow slipped *back* in time. Thousands of years by the sounds of it. She saw Graham still cowering in the ousfruit bushes. 'I'm gonna get back in my box, OK?'

'FREEZE. IF YOU PERSIST YOU WILL BE DETAINED.'

'I've done nothing wrong!'

'BOOK OF RULES CHAPTER THREE VERSE TWO: WOMANKIND IS FORBIDDEN FROM LEAVING THE HEARTH AND HOME AFTER DARK LEST SHE IS ATTENDED BY HER HUSBAND OR FATHER.'

'Oh for crying out loud!'

'VIOLATION OF HOLY LAW.'

There was a faint hum behind her and another two drones descended on the square. Yaz shot a look over her shoulder. The TARDIS was about five metres away. If she sprinted, she'd be in before the robots could respond, she was sure of it. 'I'm from off-world. I'm just a tourist. I didn't know your local laws ...' It was worth a try.

'VIOLATION OF HOLY LAW.'

Here goes nothing. Yaz turned and dived towards the TARDIS.

'ARREST IMMINENT.'

In the same instant, all the drones turned red. At first, Yaz felt like she had pins and needles all over her body, then her back arched in agony for a split second before everything went black.

Chapter 4

The town now behind them, the Doctor and Ryan made their way along the zigzag cliff paths that led up to the strange blue tower. Lanterns lit the route. The terrain was rough and rocky and, in the dark, Ryan had to take extra care of how to plant his feet. An electric blue lizard with bright orange markings scurried past him and darted into the scrub.

The tower stood at the very top of the hillside, looking out over the whole of New Town. Up close, it seemed even bigger to Ryan, ten storeys high at least – maybe more. He felt very small in comparison.

'It's the TARDIS right? It's gotta be,' he said.

'Looks like it.'

'Won't it be all locked up at this time of night?'

'Only one way to find out,' the Doctor said, undeterred. 'The lights are on, so I'm guessing someone's home. See the way they flicker? Candles. I wonder if it's a church or a temple ...'

The path eventually opened out onto a flat concourse. Sweat ran down Ryan's back from the hike. There seemed to be a main entrance flanked by grand stairs and weathered statues of some man in a long cloak. The Doctor was right, thought, Ryan – definitely a church. Above the door the word TORDOS was carved in a stone plinth.

'Tordos? TARDIS?'

The Doctor chuckled. 'That really would be a coincidence, wouldn't it?'

'What we gonna do? Just barge in?'

The Doctor shrugged. 'Why not? We've done nothing wrong. Yet.' She barrelled up the steps. Where *did* she get her energy from? Ryan was gagging for a Red Bull, frankly. She pushed on the left-hand side of the huge double doors. 'Look! Wide open for prayer and quiet contemplation!'

Ryan paused halfway up the stairs and frowned. He couldn't put his finger on it, but this didn't feel right.

Graham hardly dared to breathe. From his hiding place, he watched a buggy swerve onto the square. Was ... was Yasmin ... dead? He fought his first instinct to run towards her, knowing that he couldn't do a thing to help if they both got shot down. The floating globes continued to circle the TARDIS, scanning it with their lasers or whatever they were.

His stomach turned. What would he ... how would he ... how could he tell Mr and Mrs Khan that ...? He thought back the moment when Grace was ... How could he not? He blinked back tears.

The buggy skid to a halt and two hooded figures sprung down. All he could make out were their long coats and sturdy boots. They crouched alongside Yasmin.

'Hello?' One of them rolled her body over. 'Young woman? No good. She's unconscious. Out cold.'

Graham stifled a huge sigh of relief. She was alive.

'Good Doctor in Tordos! What on Lobos was she thinking?' said the second monk, who sounded older. Graham thought they were distinctly monk-y. 'Such brazen dress! And to be out alone at night!'

'You don't think … she's one of them? A … *rebel*?'

'To flaunt the Good Law so boldly. I wouldn't be surprised, Brother Tempika. I wouldn't be surprised in the slightest. Look at her. She could even be a … *mongrel*.'

'What should we do, Brother Glezos?'

Brother. So they *were* monks. Graham couldn't remember any monks acting like policemen earlier on.

'What else can we do? Confine her to the cells until one of the Fathers can hear her testimony and pass sentence.'

Graham watched the one called Tempika pull back his hood. He was a lad, not much older than Ryan from the looks of it, with floppy brown hair and trendy stubble. Graham crouched further into the shadows. There was no way he could take on two fit men *and* the laser globes. 'Careful!' snapped Glezos. 'She might be wearing an explosive vest.'

'I don't think she is …'

Yaz was wearing jeans and a long-sleeved T-shirt. There was nowhere she could be hiding explosives, the idiots.

'Very well. Put her on the cart.' From under the hood, Graham glimpsed dark skin and a bushy black beard. Glezos looked to the sphere closest to him. 'Eyes dismissed.'

All three of the globes drifted off in opposing directions. Graham ducked further into the bushes. Through the

29

foliage, he watched them load Yaz into the back of the buggy before boarding themselves.

It growled over the gravel, skirting almost right past his nose. As she went past, Graham saw that Yasmin looked peaceful, like she was merely sleeping. He sincerely hoped getting zapped hadn't hurt as much as it looked like it did.

The buggy turned right, downhill. Graham stuck his head through the leaves, to check that the coast was clear. New Town was still once more – no monks or spiky spheres in sight. Sticking to the shadiest part of the streets, he took off in pursuit of the cart. He wouldn't let Yaz out of his sight.

To Ryan, the Temple of Tordos smelled like the big posh church they'd done the nativity play at when they'd been at Redlands: incense and myrrh. Every year, each class trundled in a long line down the street and around the corner and all the mums and dads came to watch. Well, all except his.

The entrance hall here was beautiful, though, even if churches weren't Ryan's thing. Hundreds and hundreds of candles flickered inside jars and from gold chandeliers and candelabras. If anything, this was even grander than Sheffield Cathedral: grey marble pillars stretched to the high ceilings and the doors were gilded in gold.

The Doctor's footsteps clipped on the gleaming floors and echoed off the walls. A flight of stairs led up to big gold doors and a small archway led down some stairs into the basement.

'Female worship ...' The Doctor read the sign over the archway. 'Hmm, I don't think so. Before my last regeneration, I was allowed to go anywhere I wanted, what exactly has changed?' She indignantly started up the stairs towards what Ryan guessed was the main chapel.

'Doctor? Do you think we should be doing this?'

'Oh it's fine! It's quite beautiful, don't you think? Bit OTT maybe. I remember saying to Michelangelo when he was doing the Sistine ... I said, "Mikey, love, less is more sometimes." Look at these though ... familiar.' She gestured at the wood carvings adorning the walls. Each of them seemed to depict the TARDIS in some way. In one, winged angels flew from their time machine.

'They think angels came out of the TARDIS? Seriously, though? What's going on?'

'I'm not sure yet.' She stopped her ascent for a moment. 'Let's assume the TARDIS jolted forwards in time. It seems that our involvement in the peace treaty has become the foundation of a religion.'

Ryan jogged up the stairs to catch her. 'And ... that's OK?'

The Doctor chewed her lip. 'It's not *ideal*. Time Lords have strict rules about intervention, but it's not the first time this has happened.' Every once in a while, Ryan noticed the Doctor slipped into History Lesson Mode. He quite liked it. He used to like History, it was miles better than Maths. 'There was a time, Ryan, when the Time Lords were feared and adored in equal measure, across all of time and space. It's a heady feeling, knowing people regard you as both gallant protector and capricious tyrant.' The candlelight glimmered like amber in her green eyes.

'Like gods?'

She paused. 'No. Not like gods.' She continued towards the chapel.

'Sound like gods to me.'

'Hmm,' she said. 'A few of us thought so. Never ended well for them, mind you.' They reached the gilded doors. She gave a gentle knock. 'No one home.'

She twisted the handle and pushed the door wide.

Graham followed the cart at a safe distance. Every few metres he ducked behind a dustbin or the strange blue columns most of the houses seemed to have on their doorsteps. Rats the size of racoons and with tails like whips darted through the gutters.

There were no other vehicles on the roads so it wasn't difficult to keep track of them. Not for the first time since meeting the Doctor, he thought he was getting fitter. Beating cancer had been a major wakeup call to watch his health, but since chasing around after the Doctor all day, he swore he'd lost about half a stone without even giving up Gregg's pasties.

The buggy bumped over the cobbles all the way to the bottom of the hill and into the harbour. The weirdest thing was, thought Graham, that they'd been down here to that taverna a few hours ago, but everything looked different. The streets were neater, lined with lanterns. The taverna had a fresh red sign hanging over the door. Any signs of the civil war seemed to have been tidied away very quickly.

Graham stuck to the shadows, scurrying from doorway to doorway. He reached the bottom of the hillside and was hit by a fresh wave of harbour odours: salt air and a fishy pong from the nets which were hung out, drying overnight. The boats clinked against their moorings and he had a sudden strange homesickness for his childhood ... summer holidays to Margate or Whitstable.

The buggy came to a stop before some serious-looking gates. Graham couldn't really make out what was behind them, but it was guarded like a fortress. These must be the cells the monks were talking about. He ducked behind an old row boat. This could be his only chance to save Yaz. He'd wait for the buggy to go through the gates and slip through behind them, hopefully unnoticed, and then ... well ... He'd cross that bridge when he came to it.

Brother Tempika typed in a code and the gates started to grind open.

This was it. Graham darted forward. *Not bad for a bloke my age*, he thought. The buggy crunched over the gravel and the gates started to close behind it. 'Oh no you don't, you beggar ...' Graham hissed.

'HALT.'

Oh ... bother.

Graham froze, skidding over the rough terrain.

'IDENTIFY.'

Hands over his head, Graham turned to face the spiky drone that hovered over him.

'Sorry mate ... I was just trying to help my ...'

The light inside the drone flickered over him. 'ERROR. RETRY SCAN.'

'I ... I don't want no trouble, I just ...'

'IDENTIFIED. THE GOOD DOCTOR.'

The main chapel was as black as night. Ryan could hardly see his hand at the end of his arm. The Doctor held out her sonic screwdriver and it emitted an orange firefly of white light.

'Give me a sec,' she said. 'There's gotta be a light switch somewhere ... and if there isn't ...'

The resonance of the screwdriver changed pitch and the main lights in the hall flickered on.

'Oh ... Wow.' It was even more impressive than Ryan had imagined. The high ceiling was held up by gold columns. He looked up, craning his neck. The ceiling was decorated with some sort of mural: more angels with vast white wings spilled from what was clearly supposed to be the TARDIS.

He chuckled. 'Doctor ... like what is going on? For real?' He looked around. She'd vanished. She was always doing that. 'Doctor?'

'I'm over here.' Her voice was strained. Something was up.

Ryan followed her voice through the middle of the pews towards the altar. 'What is it?'

She was standing before a lavish gold pulpit which in turn stood before an enormous stained-glass window. 'Ryan ...' She was as white as a very white sheet. 'This is a bit unexpected.'

Ryan stumbled, looking over his shoulder. 'I don't get it.'

'Look!' The Doctor pointed the sonic at the mighty window and another light blasted on. Ryan saw the whole thing properly for the first time. He inhaled sharply. There was no mistaking it. The stained glass depicted a man, an older man, his arms spread wide and a fatherly smile on his face.

It was *nuts* but it looked *exactly* like Graham. Like, seriously.

'Oh, Ryan.' She turned to face him. 'I honestly can't decide if this is terrible ... or *brilliant*.'

'It's Graham ...'

'I know!' She smiled broadly. 'Come on! I'm thinking we should probably slip away into the night and leave Lobos to it.'

'Yeah? Shouldn't we tell them that Graham isn't ... like a god or whatever?'

She shook her head. 'There's planets out there worshipping a *lot* worse than Graham O'Brien, believe you me.' She danced down the steps leading to the altar and started down the aisle. Ryan hurried to catch her up.

'It's the church of *Graham*! That's mad!'

'He's a good egg!'

'But still ... he's not a god. He's a retired bus driver!'

'This is ... an *unexpected* side effect of our last trip.' The Doctor paused for a moment to think. 'But I think undoing the last trip would cause more damage than good. One day, when we're really, especially bored, I'll explain about paradoxes. Although, to be fair, sometimes they are quite funny. And then, another time, I'll tell you everything they got wrong in *Back to the Future*.'

She resumed her march towards the exit.

'We didn't ask them to do all this, Ryan! We were just doing the right thing … and if Lobos wants to follow our example of peace and tolerance, well …'

The Doctor flung the door open and was confronted by a vicious floating ball. 'Uh oh!'

It was sort of like the Urbankan one Ryan and Yaz had fetched from the TARDIS, but this one was covered in spikes. It looked far less friendly.

'Hello there …' the Doctor said, staggering backwards into the aisle. She bumped into Ryan.

'HALT,' a robotic voice said. 'IDENTIFY.'

'I am the Doctor and this is Ryan Sinclair.'

White laser beams flickered from the ball, seemingly scanning them.

'VIOLATION OF HOLY LAW.'

'What?' Ryan said.

'Oh that's never good,' the Doctor added.

'BOOK OF WORSHIP. CHAPTER TWO, VERSE THIRTEEN. "LO! THE TEMPLE OF TORDOS IS MY HOME," SAID THE GOOD DOCTOR. "ALL HUMANS SHALL HAVE A HOME IN THE TEMPLE WHERE MENFOLK AND LOWLY WOMENFOLK MUST WORSHIP APART."'

The Doctor bit her lip. 'Ah well that explains the whole *women in the basement* sign we saw, then.'

'Lowly?' Ryan said with faint disgust. 'Shade.'

The drone continued to pursue them down the aisle. 'This is a mistake,' the Doctor said with sudden authority. 'Scan me again. I'm not loba or human. I'm not man *or* woman in the way you understand it. Scan me again!'

It did so. 'HOLY VIOLATION.'

'Great. Another one.'

'BOOK OF TRUTHS. CHAPTER ONE, VERSE EIGHT. HUMANS ARE MADE IN THE IMAGE OF THE GOOD DOCTOR. THEY ARE LIVING PROOF OF HIS PUREST DESIGN AND LIFE MOST HOLY. TO DISTORT THE PURITY OF THE GOOD DOCTOR IS AN ABOMINATION.'

'Ryan. Shall I tell you what never ends well?'

'Go on ...'

'Literally *any* sort of chat about racial "purity". We need to get out.' She grabbed Ryan's arm and sprinted underneath the drone towards the door.

'HALT.'

They ran out of the chapel to the top of the stairs, only to see another four drones gliding up the staircase towards them.

'Doctor ...'

'Back inside!' She pushed him back through the doors. 'Help me!'

They took a door each, sealing them inside with the first drone.

'THE TEMPLE OF TORDOS IS DEFILED. THE PUNISHMENT BY HOLY LAW IS DEATH.'

'No!' the Doctor protested.

'As if!' Ryan cried.

'HOLY LAW IS ABSOLUTE.'

The floating ball turned from pale green to dark red. It glowed brighter and the Doctor howled in pain.

'Doctor!' Ryan yelled. 'Stop! Stop it!'

Her body shook and convulsed, surrounded by the same blood-red haze. She crumpled to her knees, her face contorted in agony. Ryan tried to help her, but the red light punched his hand back like it was made of static electricity. He fell back clutching his fingers.

'Doctor!'

The Doctor curled up in a ball. There was nothing Ryan could do but watch. It was killing her.

Chapter 5

'Somebody help!' Ryan howled. 'Just stop!'

He wasn't sure if it was listening or not, but suddenly, the drone changed colour: from scarlet to amber. 'EMERGENCY OVERRIDE. ALL EYES CONVERGE AT TEMPLE.'

The Doctor rolled flat on her back with a sigh.

Ryan threw himself at her side and lifted her up. 'Doctor? Doctor are you OK? Oh, mate …'

The Doctor groaned like her alarm had gone off at six AM. 'Owwwwwwww,' she said, stretching. 'That wasn't very nice, now, was it?'

Ryan exhaled like he'd never exhaled before. She was fine. Although she did smell slightly like burned toast.

'Oof. That reminds me of this time I had a deep tissue massage on Crandulox-7. By that I mean tiny nanobots actually burrow deep into your tissue and … What are they doing?' She suddenly sat bolt upright, fighting fit.

The doors burst open, clattering into the walls. Ryan watched as five more amber spiked drones glided into the chapel. 'I dunno. It just went orange and stopped.'

'THE TIME IS UPON US.' All of the drones – the Eyes – all spoke in unison. 'THE TIME IS UPON US.'

'Divine intervention?' The Doctor clutched Ryan and rose to her feet, shaking it off.

The Eyes continued to drift into the Temple, all chanting. In the middle of them, his arms up in surrender, came a sheepish-looking Graham.

'Oh, thank god for that!' he said. 'There you are! These things have gone barking mad!'

Ryan looked behind him at the stained-glass window featuring his nan's husband. 'Erm, yeah. There's a lot of that going on.'

The Doctor held out her arm. 'Come here. I think it's safe.'

Graham ran to her side.

'What happened?' she asked.

'This has gone properly pear-shaped, Doctor. First they took Yaz …'

Her face fell. 'Who did?'

'Them! The world's scariest flying footballs!'

'Well, where did they take her? Is she all right?'

'I dunno! They used a stun ray on her or something. She's alive, but they took her to some prison down the bottom of the hill.'

The Doctor puffed her cheeks out. 'I often wonder *why*. Why do I travel through time and space? And I often think it's on the off-chance that one day I'll tell my chums to wait in the TARDIS and they'll actually *listen*.' She cupped Graham's face and looked him in the eye. 'What about you? Did they hurt you?'

'No. No it's weird. They keep saying *I'm* the Doctor …'

The Doctor's eyes widened. 'Oh. OK. Makes sense.'

'Aw, that might explain that then …' Ryan stepped aside and Graham saw the giant window for the first time.

'Oh. My. Days. What is *that*?'

'Well …' the Doctor said. 'It's either you or him from that gameshow. But that would be ridiculous, so the odds are …'

Ryan thought Graham looked rather pale.

'But … but that's …'

'It was always foretold that the Good Doctor would return.' A new voice echoed throughout the Temple.

The Doctor, Ryan and Graham turned to face the arrival. He was an old, bald man with a beaky nose that gave him a decidedly birdlike appearance. He wore a gold, floor-length coat, with bloomers and suspenders, just like the Doctor's, but infinitely more regal with an intricate question-mark motif embroidered on the collar. He was followed into the chapel by two men dressed similarly, but with hoods covering most of their heads, like monks.

The newcomer approached the trio with great ceremony and deference, falling to his knees before Graham, bowing his forehead all the way to the floor. 'I never doubted it, O Good Doctor. My faith was strong, and you have come back to us.'

Graham stooped down to pick him up. 'There's no need for that, mate. Up you get. Seriously. Anyway, I'm not …'

The man – a priest, Ryan guessed – clung to Graham's hand like his life depended on it. 'It's you. It's truly *you*. The great inferno of 270PD destroyed so many of the relics from that time, but a single image survived ... and it's *you*!'

'Um, yeah, OK. And you are?'

'I'm so sorry, allow me to introduce myself: I am High Priest Mykados, your most humble servant.'

The Doctor stepped between Mykados and Graham and prodded the High Priest squarely in the chest. 'Never mind that. Your little robot guard dogs almost gamma-rayed me to death. What's that about?'

Mykados looked horrified, but Ryan noted he pretty much ignored the Doctor, speaking directly to Graham. 'Oh, I beg your mercy. The Eyes are programmed to protect the Temple at all costs. As you know, my all-seeing benevolent lord, these are violent times on Lobos. But all of the Eyes are programmed to recognise this face ...' He reached for Graham's cheek, as if he was unable to believe he was really there in the flesh.

Graham ducked away. 'Erm, yeah, that's my face, mate.'

'And on the eve of the St Rasmin's Day! Praise be!' Mykados held his palms to the sky.

St Rasmin? *No way*, thought Ryan, *Ryan and Yasmin ...*

'Happy St Rasmin Day and all that,' said the Doctor. 'But lo! Massive fail! Your "Eyes" have taken one of the Good Doctor's ... disciples ... to your jail.'

'Yes!' Graham agreed. 'They took Yaz!'

Mykados looked deeply panicked. 'I apologise profusely. Once more I can only beg your divine forgiveness, almighty one. The Eyes are set to maximum security so close to the feast, but rest assured your acolyte shall be freed at once.'

The Doctor seemed to relax a little. 'Good! That's more like it. But we do need to talk about this whole No Women In The Church thing. What's that about? Tell 'em, Good Doctor.' She gave Graham a nudge.

'What? Oh right, fair enough. Yeah. You should ... let women in the church. Obviously.'

Mykados looked momentarily horrified before nodding profusely. 'If you will it, so shall it be.'

Ryan tried to catch the Doctor's eye. Pretending that Graham, of all people, was a god wasn't gonna end well, was it? He'd sat through enough charades last Christmas to know that Graham was a very, very bad actor. All he could think was that the Doctor felt it was worth playing along until they could make a swift exit.

Mykados turned back to one of the monks. 'Brother Alexis, please send word to the monastery that the glorious news is true! Tell Father Panos that the Good Doctor walks among us once more and that the Feast of St Rasmin is cancelled for worship.'

'Oh no, don't do that on my account,' Graham said. 'I bet people were quite looking forward to that.'

Mykados bowed his head. 'As you wish, Wondrous One. You heard His exalted word, Alexis. The feast will go ahead in His honour. Go! Go at once!'

The monk bowed his head and hurried out of the Temple.

Graham grabbed the Doctor's arm. 'Doctor, what am I supposed to do? These blokes think ...'

'Just play along until we have Yaz back safe and sound,' she hissed, speaking at a thousand miles a minute. 'He won't listen to me but I have to find out what's going on. This is, at least partly, my fault. I left the Urbankan drone behind by accident and they developed the Eyes. Graham, in advancing their technology, I broke a rule, a *massive* rule. And now I have to fix it.'

Mykados turned back to them. 'I realise as a humble human, I have no right to ask anything of you, cherished leader, but we – as your servants – would be honoured if you'd grace us with your presence at the Feast of St Rasmin …'

'Erm … this Rasmin …?' Ryan asked. 'Who's that, then?'

Mykados looked confused. 'St Rasmin was, of course, the most glorious archangel who turned off the sun on the day of the Homecoming and whose magnificent voice spoke to all the humans on Lobos.'

'Oh wow!' Ryan said with a wide smile. 'That was me, that was! Well we didn't turn off the sun so much as …'

'Never mind that, *Rasmin*,' said the Doctor, cutting him off. 'High Priest Mykados, may I ask how long it's been since this … Homecoming?'

The younger monk stepped forward. 'It is forbidden for womenfolk to directly address the High Priest. Their tongues speak lies and spread disease.'

The Doctor blinked, aghast.

'You what?' Graham said. 'Who came up with that claptrap?'

'You, my magnificence,' the monk said.

'It's recorded in the Book of Truths,' Mykados explained. 'It was the women who brought about the fall, the great plague. They betrayed your word and carry the weight of the Endless Sin.'

'Oh that sounds fun,' the Doctor mused.

'Tell you what,' Graham said. 'What if the Endless Sin … ends? Right now! I … let the women off the hook. The Doctor …' Graham realised at the last second that if he was the Doctor, the Doctor would need to be someone else. '… says because I am the Good Doctor.'

Nice save, thought Ryan. Maybe Graham actually had this.

'And from now on,' Graham went on. 'I instruct you to talk to my friend … the Nurse.'

'The Nurse?' the Doctor exploded.

'What's wrong with nurses?'

The Doctor relented but didn't look wildly impressed. 'Good point, well made. I'm the Nurse.'

Mykados finally looked the Doctor, the real one, in the eye. 'Our scripture says nothing of the Nurse.'

'I'd like a little look at this scripture of yours,' the Doctor said, now deadly serious. Her eyes narrowed. 'But first, we need to collect our other little angel from your jail.'

Chapter 6

Yasmin Khan had never had a hangover, but, if she *had*, she suspected it'd probably feel like this. It was as if her brain was banging on the inside of her skull trying to get out.

Just for a second, she thought she was tucked up in bed at home. Then she woke in panic that she was late for a shift. And then she remembered where she was.

She wasn't outside the TARDIS any more. The first thing that hit her was the *smell*. Wherever she was reeked of damp, cheesy feet, sewage and body odour all at the same time. Her hand flew over her mouth and nose, trying to block out the stench with the sleeve of her jersey.

She was laid flat on her back, on a cold, hard surface. Ready to defend herself, she shot upright, only to bump her head on the top bunk. 'Ow!'

'Mind your head,' said a gruff voice.

The cell – and Yaz had seen enough of those to know she was in one – was foul, dank and dirty. The walls were dripping with water and she could hear the ocean beyond the high window bars. Yaz subscribed to the old adage that you can judge a society based on how it treats its prisoners and, frankly, she was judging Lobos pretty badly right now.

Four sets of bunk beds were jammed in the small cell block, but there were two other inmates by the looks of things.

'Rough night?' the loba opposite her said. He had black fur, speckled with silver. He was laid casually on his back, hands under his head like a pillow. 'You're in Old Town jail.'

Yaz rubbed her head. 'Those sphere things …'

'The Eyes. Yeah. Hurt like hell if they stun you.' The inmates, Yaz noticed, were both loba. The other one seemed to be passed out in a drunken stupor above the other one on the top bunk. 'Which holy law did you break?'

Her vision kept swimming in and out of focus. 'The "being a girl" one.'

The loba bared his fangs in what was probably a smile. 'Oh dear. They don't like that one little bit.'

'I was out by myself at night, apparently that's a crime.'

'What were you selling?'

'Nothing!' Yaz said defiantly. 'I'm … not from this planet.'

Now he sat up, swinging his legs off the bunk. 'Liar.'

'I'm not lying!'

'The spaceport has been closed for almost a hundred years.'

Yaz looked around the cell. Moonlight filtered in from the windows. There was no way she was fitting through those bars. Escape wasn't an option. 'Yeah, well we

48

didn't arrive via the spaceport. Look, what's going on here? The last time … erm … the last thing I heard about Lobos was that there'd been a truce between the humans and loba.'

He snorted through his snout. 'There was never a truce.'

'There was!' Yaz said indignantly. 'It was brokered by Orryx and Blaine. I was … I read about it.'

He rubbed a slim metal collar around his neck, loosening it. 'Well, I've never heard of any Orryx or a truce, but Blaine was one of the founding fathers. Don't know what you've been reading.'

Yaz frowned. 'What are you talking about? Orryx was the leader of the Loba Army. There was a civil war between loba and humans and then the Doctor helped them to draw up a power-sharing scheme where …'

'Shut up right now! Are you insane?' he growled, his eyes blazing in the murk. 'You'll get us all killed with talk like that. It's heresy.'

Oh wow. The TARDIS must have really, really badly missed the spot this time. From the way this guy was talking, they must be hundreds, if not thousands, of years in the future. If he'd heard of Blaine, she guessed it couldn't be the past. Something had gone wrong with Lobos too. Loba in collars and chains wasn't part of the peace deal they'd helped to write.

'Sorry,' she said. 'I'm Yaz.'

'They call me Seadog Bob.'

'What are you in for?'

'I was caught without my master.'

'What?'

His ice-blue eyes narrowed. 'Loba must not roam public spaces without their human. S'why we call this place "the Pound".'

'That's ridiculous,' Yaz said.

'Again, be careful what you're saying. It's holy law. I can't work out if you're brave or stupid.'

Yaz smiled. Before she met the Doctor, that comment would have really upset her. Now, not so much. 'Little bit of both probably,' she said, because she thought that's what the Doctor would say. 'Will they let us go?'

'You maybe. You're human. If they don't track down my master, I'll be put down.'

'Put down?'

'Maybe you really are a bit simple.' Seadog Bob held her gaze. 'Exterminated.'

Yaz's eyes widened in horror. *What on earth has happened here?*

A team of monks arrived at the Temple of Tordos on little golf buggies – at least that's what they looked like to Ryan – to take them to collect Yaz. The Doctor, Graham and Mykados rode on one, while Ryan was relegated to riding with a younger, hooded monk who introduced himself as Brother Tempika. He looked a bit hipster with his floppy hair and neat beard.

They bumped over the cobbles, downhill towards the coast. The streets of what they *now* called Old Town were narrow and haphazard, with washing lines zigzagging from the ramshackle houses. It seemed wherever you were in the town, you could see the Temple looming over you.

A couple of times, Tempika seemed so transfixed by his passenger that he came close to steering them into ditches. 'You wanna keep your eyes on the road, mate,' Ryan said, gripping the buggy.

'Forgive me, St Rasmin.' His hands seemed to be trembling.

Ryan felt bad for snapping. 'Hey it's cool. We're all good. And just call me Rasmin.'

'This day.' Tempika said, blushing slightly. 'Every day for as long as I remember, I've been waiting for this day. We knew the Good Doctor would return if we were pure of heart and faith. He has rewarded us.'

'Yeah?' Ryan said. 'Your Book of Truths … what does it say the reward is?'

'That the Good Doctor will return and save us all from our earthly torment.'

'Here? It doesn't look so bad!'

Tempika shook his head sadly. 'The quiet is deceptive, my lord. This conflict … the Temple and the rebels. Much innocent blood has been spilled, St Rasmin. He must be so disappointed in us.' He gestured at the buggy ahead. Graham looked over his shoulder and gave Ryan a wink.

'What? "The Good Doctor"? Nah, he's sound.' Ryan wondered what conflict Tempika meant. Earlier on, and however many centuries ago, it had been humans versus loba. Now it was the Temple versus rebels. *Man, why can't people just get along?* That was a point, actually: where *were* all the loba? Tonight, Ryan had only seen humans.

'St Rasmin? Dare I ask a question?'

51

'Knock yourself out. Wait! Not literally. Keep driving in a straight line.'

'The Book of Truths speaks of the Good Doctor's immense powers – how he was able to fly through space and time. Why now does he need to ride a cart?'

'Well,' Ryan said. 'Erm … when he's … moving among humans … he likes to blend in.'

'Ah, I see. We are not worthy of his love.'

Ryan laughed, imagining Graham flying through the sky like Superman. 'Don't beat yourself up about it. This time, literally.'

Up ahead, the buggy carrying the Doctor and Graham skidded to an abrupt halt. The Doctor leapt off the vehicle the second it stopped. Tempika pulled up alongside it.

'What's up?' Ryan called over to the Doctor who was now running across the empty square.

'The TARDIS!' She spun back to face them, her coat tails flapping. 'It's gone!'

Chapter 7

Graham looked around and realised this was the same fruit grove where the TARDIS had landed.

'A blue box?' The Doctor turned to Mykados. 'There was a blue box right here.' There was even a square impression of where the TARDIS had stood in the dust.

'Just as in the Book of Truths,' said Tempika, eyes wide.

Mykados ignored the Doctor and instead spoke to Graham. 'You returned to us in the blue box, just as legend foretold.'

'Yep!' Graham said. 'And now it's gone!'

'Use the Eyes,' the Doctor said. 'They patrol the streets, don't they? They'll show us who took it.'

Mykados once more looked to Graham, who scowled and answered, 'Do as she says!'

'Very well.' He spoke to one of the hooded monks. 'Brother Takis, return to the Temple and access the Eye database. See what you can find out. Good Doctor, this could only be the actions of the rebel forces.'

'What rebels?' the Doctor asked.

'Blasphemous heathens. Those who question your Word, Good Doctor.'

Graham looked to the Doctor for help. This being a god bit was starting to wear a bit thin, truth be told. 'Doc … Nurse. It'll be all right, though, yeah? The TARDIS?'

The Doctor rolled her eyes. 'Oh, the old girl's been through worse. She's indestructible … more or less. But it's no less annoying that it's been towed. Why is it every planet in the cosmos has flipping traffic wardens, eh?'

Graham realised that this Mykados chap was only gonna jump if he said so. 'Listen, mate. We're gonna really need that box back, yeah? It contains … great gifts and stuff.'

Mykados fell to Graham's feet. 'Please forgive us, O Mighty One. Please understand the vast majority of people on Lobos are devoted to exalting your name. Moving your sacred icon is highest sacrilege. When we find the rebels who dared to lay their hands on it, I assure you their hands will be removed.'

'Crikey, mate. There'll be no need for that. We just want it back, that's all.' Graham crouched to help Mykados up. 'Up you get.'

Behind him, the Doctor looked very grim indeed. 'When we get our friend out of jail, High Priest Mykados, we need to have a little sit down and chat about your Book of Truths.'

Graham nodded along.

'Whatever you wish.'

'The thing is … I'm wondering how many truths are in it. Come on! One thing at a time. Let's get Yaz and then the TARDIS! Off we go!' Graham had seen the steely look in the Doctor's eyes before. Underneath her warm smile, she was getting very, very angry.

Yaz prodded the tray of food that had been slid through the hatch in the door with a spork. Perhaps appropriately, it looked like dog food: meaty lumps in gravy. She put it to one side.

'I'd eat that, if I were you,' Bob said through mouthfuls. 'Tastes of dirt but it's all you'll get until tomorrow.'

'I won't be here tomorrow,' Yaz said. 'This is all a mix-up. I shouldn't be here.'

'Girl out by herself at night. That's five lashes from one of the sisters, that is.'

'What? What happened here, Bob? It … wasn't always like this. So I read,' she added quickly.

His eyes narrowed. 'Oh don't start all that again. I told you. The Temple of Tordos has ruled for hundreds of years. It's all any of us know. Sure we have the army and each major town has a mayor, but it all trickles down from that blue eyesore on the hill. Mykados and his cronies pull all the puppet strings.'

Yaz didn't know what any of that meant and she didn't want to raise further suspicions by asking a ton of questions, so she nodded solemnly.

Their other cellmate, another, older loba with one eye had arisen from his bunk when the food arrived. 'If I wasn't so old, I'd be down the mines, I would.'

Bob growled. 'Quiet you old fool! Unless you want them to take your other eye.'

'What's down the mines?' Yaz asked.

'The rebels,' the old dog said. 'More power to 'em, I say. They got the church worried, they have.'

'He don't know what he's talking about,' Bob said, scraping the last drops of his slop out of the dish. 'You not eating that? I'll have it if it's going.'

There was a commotion from outside the cell. A howl so loud and pained that Yaz had to cover her ears. 'What *is* that?'

Bob rolled his eyes. 'Tromos is awake.'

Yaz clambered up onto the top bunk to see through the bars into the corridor beyond. If she clung to the bars and stood on tiptoes, she could see out into an equally dank corridor. Opposite her cell was an identical one from which came the guttural cries. 'It hurts! It hurts!' Vast paws, more like a *bear* than a dog, gripped the bars in the door, although Yaz couldn't see the rest of him. The whole corridor seemed to rattle as he shook the bars.

'Who's Tromos?' she asked.

Bob shook his head sadly. 'It ain't right what they did to him.'

'Let me out!' Tromos roared. 'Let me out! The pain!'

'What did they do? Is he OK?'

'You ask too many questions.'

'It's my job to ask questions.' She hopped down and sat back on her bunk. 'So?'

'About a decade back. The Temple did experiments on loba. Supposed to be creating guards, so they said, but we all know they were trying to build an army to crush the rebellion. We're bigger, stronger, than humans. Makes sense I guess. "Guard dogs".'

'And he's one of them?'

Pity and sadness filled Bob's eyes. 'Poor old Tromos. Last one left alive. They pumped them full of drugs, all sorts of surgeries to make 'em strong, fast, aggressive. But they all went mad, didn't they. The others all killed themselves … or had to be exterminated.'

Across the hall, Tromos continued to hurl himself against the door. 'It hurts!'

The old dog finished his second bowl of goo. 'They keep him sedated in here mostly.'

Yaz shook her head. 'That's barbaric. They can't do that.'

'That's the Temple for you.'

Tromos howled like a wolf.

'Poor guy,' Yaz said.

A bird hooted outside the external window and Yaz wondered if dawn was on the horizon. Only then Bob put his paws to his muzzle and made a birdlike whistle in response.

She stared at him and waited for an explanation. He didn't offer one readily. 'What? You speak bird?' Yaz said.

'More questions?'

She smiled. 'Always.'

'Never mind questions. If you know what's good for you, you'll take cover.'

Outside, the bird warbled again.

'Huh?'

'Right now!' Bob threw himself to the floor, rolling underneath his bunk and Yaz quickly followed suit. In the corridor, she heard a metallic clink. She was no expert, but it sounded, she guessed, like a grenade.

The second her shoulder hit the cell floor, the whole room seemed to quake. The blast was so loud, her ears felt like they were exploding. Masonry rained down on her hair and back and she scrambled under her bunk. She screwed her eyes shut and waited for some kind of pain to strike.

Only it never came.

She felt someone tugging on her arm. Her ears ringing, she dared to open her eyes to see Bob dragging her off the ground through a fog of thick black dust and smoke. She tried to ask what was going on, but she was totally deaf.

She saw his mouth moving. 'Get up! Get up now!' Her hearing started to return over a high-pitched, pealing sound. He sounded very quiet, like when you're coming in to land on an aeroplane. 'If you want to live, you'll come with me! NOW!'

Through the dust, she saw there was now a gaping hole in side of the cell. A whole wall had collapsed. 'What's going on?'

'No more questions! Move!' Bob yanked her so hard, her arm almost came out of its socket. Finding her feet, Yaz climbed over the rubble and into the corridor.

'What about him?' She pointed to the grizzled old loba in the cell.

'He's lame, he'll slow us down,' Bob shouted.

Yaz knew the Doctor would never leave someone behind. She turned to him. 'Come with us!'

His one eye widened. 'Are you mad, human? You'll all be shot on sight!'

Yaz shook her head. What choice did she have? She had to find the Doctor and make sure Graham wasn't hurt. 'Wait for me!' she called back to Bob before clambering over the heap of debris.

A human woman in a gasmask greeted them in the corridor. She thrust a gasmask at Bob. 'Pry! The sewer! This way!' Her voice was muffled by the mask. She saw Yaz for the first time. 'Who the Hades is this?'

'She's on our side.' Bob looked back at her. 'I hope. She's definitely not with the Temple.'

'Good enough for me.'

Bob and the woman charged towards the end of the corridor. Alarms sounded and Yaz heard gunfire in the distance, but getting closer.

Another noise – a low, pitiful whine. 'Help me! Get me out! It hurts!' It was Tromos. His cell, as far as she could tell, was undamaged by the blast.

Yaz peeked through the bars in his door. She couldn't see him in the dark and dust. 'Wait!' She yelled down the corridor to her rescuers. 'Shouldn't we get this guy out too?'

Bob turned back. His eyes widened. 'Come away from—'

Yaz felt the claw before she saw it. An arm punched through the bars and grabbed her around her neck. In the split second before she was pinned to the door, she saw only a glimpse of wild yellow eyes and black fur. The arm was vice-strong, powerful, muscular. Yaz sunk her fingernails into matted fur, but it made no difference.

'Little girls …' His breath smelled of rotten meat, hot on her cheek.

She couldn't cry out. Her eyes bulged. Her feet dangled helplessly above the floor as Tromos tried to pull her into his cell.

She couldn't breathe.

He was going to crush her to death.

Chapter 8

You could hear the klaxons from halfway down the hill. Ryan's heart plummeted. Alarm bells were never good. As the monk's golf cart things swung into the harbour, he saw a tower of black smoke billowing from what looked like a fortress jutting out into the sea. As they drew nearer, he was pretty sure he heard gunfire too. Even worse. 'What's going on?' he asked Tempika.

His companion was pale-faced. 'I ... I don't know.'

Up ahead, the Doctor sprung off her buggy and ran towards the prison.

'Stop! Stop her!' Mykados called. 'It's not safe!'

A fleet of what Ryan guessed were prison guards ran to greet them. They all wore functional uniforms in what could only be described as 'TARDIS Blue'. Two of them caught hold of the Doctor and held her back.

'Lads! Sorry but you need to let me go! My friend is in there!'

'Hold on now, he says it might not be safe!' Graham protested.

'Well, duh!'

'High Priest Mykados.' One of the guards bowed his head.

'What … what manner of horrors awaits?'

'Rebel attack, Your Grace. Grenade. Foot-soldiers with guns. We can't access the East Wing.'

'Tromos …?'

'We don't know, Your Grace.'

Mykados suddenly looked very worried and Ryan wondered why.

'Where was Yaz? Yasmin Khan?' the Doctor demanded.

The guards looked confused.

'Brown girl!' Ryan said urgently. 'Human! Pink trainers!'

One of the guards lowered his gaze. 'She was being held on the East Wing.'

Yaz couldn't breathe. She tried to prise Tromos's arm off her neck but it was like steel. Silvery, glittery stars swam in her peripheral vision. Everything started to go black.

And then she fell to the floor in a heap. She gasped for air, looked up, and saw Bob standing over her, some sort of stun gun in his hand. 'Get up!' he shouted. 'Can you walk?'

Yaz nodded, although she was far from certain. Her throat throbbed. Bob and the woman helped her up. 'Put this on,' the woman said, pulling a gasmask over her head. Yaz couldn't speak.

'What's her name?'

'Yaz,' Bob replied.

Through the murk, Yaz allowed the pair to guide her down the corridor.

'Yaz? Yaz can you hear me?' the woman shouted through her mask.

Yaz nodded.

'We're going into the sewer system. You need to drop down and then crawl through a narrow tunnel. Can you do that?'

Again, Yaz just nodded.

'Follow me.' The woman slid into a manhole, feet first. She lowered herself down until she was hanging onto the rim by her fingertips and then let herself drop.

The hole looked black and deep, like staring down a well. Yaz hoped the fall wasn't far. At the same time, the gunshots seemed to be getting closer and she had no desire to be caught in the crossfire. She had little choice but to go with Bob.

'Hurry up!' Bob barked.

Yaz did as the woman had done. She sat on the edge of the drain and lowered herself down.

'Drop!' the woman's voice echoed up. 'It's not that deep.'

Yaz closed her eyes and let go. There was a horrible second of freefall before she landed in something freezing cold and wet. She staggered over and fell on her bottom. She was down and nothing – new – hurt. That was good. The stench was *much* less good, and that was through a gasmask. 'Oh gross.'

'This way!' The woman shouted, already crawling through a pipe. Yaz reluctantly followed on hands and knees. The only saving grace was that it was so dark she couldn't see what she was kneeling in. With any luck this was a water overflow pipe and nothing more. Wishful thinking. The odour said otherwise. Yaz crawled as fast as she could through the narrow pipe, aware of Bob behind her. It was a tight squeeze for her, so she couldn't imagine how claustrophobic it must be for him.

'Keep going!' he growled.

All Yaz could do was wriggle forwards and hope she was going in a direction that would lead her back to the Doctor.

'Unacceptable!' The Doctor paced outside the entrance to the prison, while Graham watched on. 'Can I speak to someone in charge, please? It's so difficult when you're usually the person in charge to find someone else as in charge as you are.'

Mykados seemed much more interested in what Graham had to say. 'O Highest One, please forgive humanity's sins! Your archangel will be found. I will spare no expense or manpower until we have her back. Is this a test? Is this a test of our devotion?'

How to answer that? 'Erm, yeah. Good one. What do we do, Doc … Nurse?'

'I want her safe!' The Doctor took a deep breath before gently taking hold of Graham and Ryan's arms and leading them out of Mykados's earshot. 'Well *Highest One*, I reckon we need to – in this order – find Yaz, find the TARDIS, figure out exactly what we're supposed to have said the last time we were here, fix it, and get to Vienna in 1967 in time for Eurovision.'

Graham nodded slowly. 'Hundred per cent. Except the Eurovision bit, I'll give that a miss.'

'Really? It was the year Sandie Shaw won, but whatever.'

'Doctor!' Ryan said, exasperated.

'We've got to get inside that prison!' The Doctor darted back towards the jail at exactly the same time as some prison guards and Tempika emerged from the jailhouse. Graham hurried over to hear what they had to say.

'Report,' Mykados demanded.

'The prison is secure, Your Grace,' a guard said. 'East Wing is back under our control. A rebel is dead.'

'Tromos?'

'Secure in his cell.'

'Ah.' Mykados's shoulders went down, he took a deep breath, and Graham wondered what was so special about this Tromos fella they kept talking about. 'Praise the Good Doctor.'

The Doctor pushed forward to speak to them. 'And what about our friend? The *Archangel*?'

The guard looked shamefaced. 'We can't find her.'

'What?'

'She's gone,' Tempika said. 'One of the prisoners reports that she fled with a loba and a human rebel. Your Grace … The rebels went to such lengths to free him that we think a stray loba we picked up on the streets last night may have been important to the resistance.' A pause. 'It may have even been Pry.'

Graham saw Mykados's eyes widen and nostrils flare. 'Do you mean to tell me we had *Pry* in custody and you let him escape?'

The most senior guard fell to his knees, bowing his head all the way to the floor. 'I beg forgiveness, Your Grace. He gave a false name. We just thought he was a stray.'

'You're forgiven!' Graham interrupted loudly. He couldn't stand to see the guard scraping on the floor in his name. 'Get up, mate. There's no need to grovel.'

The guard thanked him almost tearfully.

'Good Doctor?' the real Doctor said. 'Do you think, in your infinite wisdom and awesome cleverness, we could sit down with our high priest and see if we can find out what's going on with these rebels? *Peacefully*. Before anyone gets hurt.'

'I couldn't agree more,' Graham said. 'We need to take a breather I think. I could use a sit down.'

The Doctor nodded and spoke quietly, only to Ryan and Graham. 'I need to get my bearings and piece together when we are. And what went wrong.' The Doctor scrunched her face. 'I thought we'd done a fairly textbook Save a Civilisation from the Brink of Collapse, to be honest.'

'What about Yaz?' Ryan asked.

The Doctor chewed her lip. 'Yaz is smart and capable and has a lovely singing voice. Two of those things are more important than the other at present, but worth mentioning nonetheless. If she went with these "rebels" voluntarily, I trust her judgement. In fact, hopefully she's getting the other side of the story – and there's always two sides – as we speak.'

Graham nodded. He sometimes forgot that Yaz had been in some pretty scary situations as a copper. She'd be OK. They could work out where Yaz was before anything else got blown up. The Doctor gave him a nudge. He straightened his back, puffed out his chest and cleared his throat. 'I, The Good Doctor, command that there's no more fighting tonight on the Feast of …'

'Rasmin,' Ryan helpfully added.

'But the rebels have escaped …' the guard started to argue.

'Silence!' Mykados ordered. 'This is His Word.'

'I dunno if it's appropriate to have a big shindig, what with everything that's going on, but did you say there was some sorta feast?' Graham figured if everyone was feasting, they wouldn't be fighting.

Mykados bowed his head. 'Yes, there was to be a lavish celebration in honour of St Rasmin. It's tradition.'

'Tell me, Mykados,' the Doctor said. 'Is this Pry likely to hurt our friend?'

'No,' he conceded. 'He's the leader of the insurgents, but he's not without honour.'

The Doctor seemed to consider the facts for a second. A chill sea breeze blew through the harbour. The air was still acrid, thick with smoke. Finally, she nodded, seemingly satisfied with Mykados's answer. 'Good. I doubt my pal Rasmin here needs a whole *feast* in his honour …'

'Aw,' Ryan said quietly.

'But, High Priest Mykados, I think it's time for a *sermon*.'

Chapter 9

As the Feast of Rasmin started without him, someone on mandola playing one of his least favourite, overly jolly hymns, Mykados swept through the icy catacombs under the Temple.

The vaults were guarded by old Father Kyos, who'd long since gone blind and didn't so much mind spending time in the dark cellars. 'Who goes there?' he said, looking up from his braille edition of the Book of Truths.

'It is I,' Mykados said.

'Your Grace. Happy St Rasmin's Day.'

'And to you. May I enter?'

With no further ado, Kyos entered the intricate code to unlock the Great Vault. He might've been blind, but he was a sharp as a needle. The huge doors opened with a hiss.

'Thank you, Father Kyos. I won't be a moment.' Mykados entered the torch-lit vault. In the centre of the circular room was a simple glass case. Sealed within was the Image. It was a scrap, really, a sepia-tinged fragment of a centuries-old photograph.

Mykados touched the glass cabinet. He narrowed his eyes, squinting at the picture. There was no doubting it. The man in the photograph *was* the man presently eating upstairs. 'Hmmm,' he muttered.

He crossed to a safe within the vault. He drew a key from inside his robe and unlocked it, before sliding a leather ledger off the inner shelf. He tucked that safely inside his robe before locking it again.

On his way out, he paused at Kyos's booth. 'Father Kyos? Has anyone else tried to access the vault today?'

'No, Your Grace.'

'Good.' He nodded. 'No one enters, unless I am with them. Is that understood?'

The banqueting hall in the Temple of Tordos was every bit as beautiful as the chapel. Hundreds of candles flickered at the centre of long tables around which the monks were gathered. It was, thought Ryan, very Hogwarts. Actually it was blingier than Hogwarts: the bowls and goblets were all gold plated. The chairs were more like thrones, engraved around the edges with a TARDIS motif. Bit extra, to be honest.

'Brother Tempika!' snapped one of the older monks. 'Your questions are impertinent!'

Ryan wiped a rich, creamy tomato (probably) sauce off his bowl with a hunk of bread. Tempika had been firing questions at him ever since they had arrived back at the Temple. 'Nah, it's OK. I don't mind.'

What he *did* very much mind was that all the servers and kitchen staff were loba. They ferried stew and bread and wine to the tables quietly and efficiently, each of them wearing a slim metal collar. He wasn't a fan of that. Like when he was at college and there were more people of colour serving in the canteen and mopping the floors than there were in the lecture theatres. It had been blindingly obvious to him, less obvious to the white people, perhaps.

'The Book of Truths says that when the Good Doctor returns, he will take us all with him to Tordos to fly through time and space for all eternity,' Tempika said, wide eyed. 'But ... but what is it like, Archangel Rasmin? I can barely conceive of such wonder.'

Ryan shrugged one shoulder. 'Yeah, it's pretty sweet to be honest.'

'Sweet?' asked another monk who looked no older than thirteen or fourteen. 'Like honey? Like figs?'

'Erm no. It's ... it's ... travelling with the Doctor is *nuts*.'

'Nuts like ...'

'No! I mean ... you'll see things you can't ever imagine. OK ... I've seen singing waterfalls made of pink crystals. For real! I've seen a unicorn sanctuary – actual unicorns – on a lost moon. I've seen the Big Bang happening in front of my eyes.'

'The Big Bang?' Tempika asked.

'Erm ... actually, never mind. You might not be ready for that. Sometimes it's scary, though. I think that's the price. Maybe that's like the rule of life – you can't get the really, really good stuff without the bad. There's some really scary stuff out there, man. There's bad, mad people doing terrible things, but she – erm *we* – we try to stop that. We make things better.' Ryan looked at the loba servants in the banquet hall, waiting on human masters. 'Or at least we *try*.'

At the other end of the long table, the Doctor, Graham and Mykados were having their own private party. The Doctor smiled at Mykados. She had barely touched her stew – a rich ratatouille-like thing – Graham noted.

The Doctor had mostly been content to listen to Mykados drone on about the Book of Truths over dinner, but now it seemed she was finally ready to say her piece. 'Now, Mykkie. May I call you Mykkie? Grand. You love the Good Doctor, I love the Good Doctor, we *all* love the Good Doctor.' She patted Graham tenderly on the arm. 'But the thing about the Good Doctor is how he tries, often at great personal cost, to make a positive change in the world without claiming any praise or reward. Isn't that right, Good Doctor?'

Graham, his belly full, had slightly tuned out. 'What? Oh, right, yeah. All day long. No one likes a glory hound.'

'So, Mykkie,' she went on, 'you can see how we'd be … *surprised* at how our last visit became the basis for an entire belief and legal system. Mind blown! Poof!'

Mykados took a sip of his wine. 'The Good Doctor's blessing of Lobos changed the course of history.'

'Walk me through it. Start at the beginning,' the Doctor said. 'I can't wait to see how this turns out.'

Mykados said nothing, but looked to *him* for permission to speak. 'Do as she says. I … um … will it.'

'Very well.' Mykados sat up straighter. 'The first human settlers came to Lobos six centuries ago and set about educating and helping the savage natives. I mean the loba lived like feral animals, and very much resisted the guidance of the humans at first, but then the Good Doctor came and blessed both human and loba with his wisdom and unending love.'

The Doctor raised an eyebrow. 'And did his unending love stretch to putting the loba into servitude?'

Mykados looked surprised. 'Yes.'

'I beg your pardon?'

'It is said that the Good Doctor's final words before he left Lobos were that loba were "Man's Best Friend". The loba are descended from domestic canines, are they not? Their greatest pleasure in life is loyalty to their human masters.'

The Doctor looked to Graham, who had gone pale. 'I did say that.'

'Oh come on!' the Doctor took her feet down off the table. 'You'd have to be a ... well ... fool to take that literally. So from three words, we've enslaved half the population?'

Mykados shook his head. 'Loba make up only about a fifth of the population. I ... I am sorry. Good Doctor, you seem displeased. We have only ever tried to live by your Word.'

'I never meant ...' Graham said, reeling as the implications of such a throwaway comment sunk in. How many loba, over the years ... his stomach turned. 'I never meant nothing by it.'

'I know,' the Doctor told him. She turned back to Mykados. 'So are we to assume that these rebel forces are fighting for the liberation of loba slaves?'

'Gosh, Good Nurse, no. It runs much deeper than that. They are *terrorists*, murderers. They threaten our entire way of life. They're trying to destroy the Temple, our faith.' He looked directly at Graham. 'They're trying to end *you*.'

After crawling for what felt like eternity, Yaz saw light up ahead. The woman emerged into the night ahead of her and helped to pull Yaz out. It was still the middle of the night but they were on a sandy beach. The pipe must be some sort of storm drain or sewage overflow. Yaz was filthy, stinky and wet through, shivering in the cool night air. 'Thanks.'

'Quickly,' the woman said. She pulled her mask off and she was a strikingly beautiful woman with full lips and olive skin. 'You can take these off now. This way. We can't stay in the open for long. I'm Mariya.'

Yaz took her own gasmask off. 'Yaz.'

'And I'm Pry,' said Bob, who – evidently – wasn't Seadog Bob at all. 'Quickly. Every Temple guard in Old Town will be looking for us by now. Who else was at the prison?'

'Ramos and Daley …'

'Where are they?'

Mariya looked pained. 'Ramos got out I think. Daley …' She tailed off.

'Damn,' the loba growled. 'We can't stay here.' He took Mariya's hand in his paw and they took flight.

Yaz followed Pry and Mariya as they sprinted over the sand. They stayed low, sticking to the shadows of the sea cliffs. She was dying to ask where exactly they were running to, but she strongly sensed now was not the time for more questions.

Looking over her shoulder, Mariya ran into the surf and clambered onto the rocks. 'Up here.' She and Pry pulled Yaz up. The rocks were jagged under her wet trainers and gusts of wind whipped at her hair. If she slipped, she'd break her neck. They climbed the slick terrain, helping each other up, until they came to a slit between two boulders. Mariya slipped into the dark gap.

'In! Now!' Pry barked.

Another narrow space. Great. Yaz followed Mariya into the darkness, like she was being swallowed whole by the cliffs.

Yianna always took her time when it came to emptying the bins. The glass and paper were recycled and food waste was fed to the chickens, jinties and pigs. Moreover, she got to be out of the Temple for ten blissful minutes if she dawdled. Her family had served the monks of Tordos for generations, and while she was very grateful to the brothers for providing her with food and a warm place to live, she got to spend precious little time exploring the rest of Lobos. She'd certainly never left the confines of Old Town, although she had been to the harbour a few times to collect food from the market when her mother was sick.

'What a beautiful night,' a voice said, making Yianna jump.

Instinctively, she bared her teeth and snarled. She couldn't help it. When she turned and saw one of the holy guests standing on the stairs behind her, she fell to her knees at once. If the brothers heard she'd growled at her ... 'Pray forgiveness, O Holy One.'

'Oh get up, don't be daft.' The woman held out a hand. 'Despite anything Time Lords have said in the past, future or present, I am in no way, shape or form a god.'

Understanding none of that, Yianna looked up at the strange woman. The big moon and the little moons seemed to twinkle in her eyes. Her hair shone almost blue in the moonlight. She really did look like an angel.

'I needed a break from the monkfest,' she said. 'You don't mind if I join you out here, do you?'

'No, my lord …'

'Now, what have I just said about that?'

'I'll return to my duties.'

'No, no, no! Come sit with me a minute or two, will you?' She patted the stone step alongside her. 'What's your name?'

'Yianna.'

'Yianna what?'

'I'm loba. It's forbidden for us to have litter names.'

A dark look clouded the woman's eyes. 'Big surprise. Join me! Well, if you want to – seems like you get enough orders around here.'

Yianna perched next to her on the steps, keeping a respectful distance. She smoothed her apron and coppery fur down.

'Yianna, what's going on around here? The loba weren't always slaves.'

Well, the stranger must be a god, because no one else would dare speak such blasphemy. The last female human to challenge the laws of the Temple – Mad Christabel – was torn limb from limb in the old arena. Yianna had been about seven, and not permitted inside the arena, obviously, but it was all people spoke of for moons. 'We serve the humans.'

'But why?' She leaned in close. 'The last time I was here, this was your planet. You were free.'

Yianna shook her head. She lowered her voice. 'Please don't tell the brothers I said this ...'

'Of course I won't.'

She had no idea why she trusted the strange woman, but she did. With all her heart. 'Loba don't go to school, but sometimes we hear the school lessons when we're cleaning or cooking. They don't teach children about the days before the Good Doctor visited. They just say Lobos was a planet of savages.'

'That's not true.'

'Shhh!' Yianna lowered her voice. 'That's what my grandmother used to say before she died. She used to tell me and my brothers bedtime stories about how loba were once the proud rulers of Lobos. How we were kings and queens.' She shook her head. 'But they're just loba stories for pups. I'm not a fool.'

'I am, and it's not all that bad.' The Doctor smiled. 'The loba were not born into captivity, surely you see that?'

Yianna frowned. 'We owe the humans our lives. That's why we serve them.'

'You don't owe them anything.'

'We do! The Great Plague would have ended life on Lobos if it weren't for them.'

The smile fell from the stranger's face. 'What Great Plague?'

Yianna wondered if this Good Nurse really *was* a fool. How could an angel not know the most important part of the planet's history? 'Five hundred years ago, the humans and loba broke the First Law and the Good Doctor punished the world.'

'Uh-oh. I don't like the sound of this. Go on.'

'The fall.'

'The fall?'

'The early human settlers. Some of the women sinned and … mixed … with indigenous loba males.'

'Got you. That explains a lot.'

'It is forbidden.'

'Is it now?'

'It's in the Book of Truths. The Good Doctor was displeased and unleashed a terrible plague. Almost all of the loba and hybrids were wiped out. The planet was on the brink of collapse, until the Temple was formed and brought about our salvation.'

'Interesting. How, exactly?'

The loba shrugged. 'They brought peace and … order. They took the loba in and trained us. Gave us jobs and purpose. Our lives have meaning because of the church.'

'And that's been the way ever since?'

Yianna nodded. 'The Temple saved us all. If we follow the Word of the Good Doctor, we will continue to prosper.'

'YIANNA!' That was Rust, calling from the kitchens. She'd been out here talking for too long.

'I have to go. Excuse me.' She hurried up the stairs.

'Yes.' The Doctor pursed her lips. 'You go prosper, love.' The dark storm clouds were back in her eyes.

Chapter 10

It was the blackest black Yaz had ever known. The dancing beam of Mariya's torch was all she could see as they walked further and further into the mountain. It was cold and damp, water trickling down the walls and dripping onto her head. It was so dark, all she could do was concentrate on where she was putting her feet.

The ground beneath her feet seemed to vibrate. 'Can you feel that?' she called ahead. 'Is that an earth—'

Suddenly, the caves shook more violently and she staggered forward. Her foot slipped on wet rock. In the dark, she couldn't see where to place her hands and landed painfully on her knee. Pry went down too ahead of her. 'Ow!' she cried, grasping her leg.

Mariya retrieved her torch from where she'd dropped it. 'The tremors are getting worse.'

'We need to move further inland, towards Kanda. It isn't safe here any more.'

'Look, I know I'm asking a billion questions, but what's going on?' Yaz said. 'Where are we going? Who are you? Actually that's only three questions. Your turn.'

In the darkness, she heard Pry sigh. 'We're almost at basecamp. There, I can explain everything.' Pry pulled her up. 'Are you hurt?'

'I just scraped my knee. It's fine.' Actually that was a lie, it *really* stung, but Yaz didn't want to seem like a wimp. 'Let me start, then. I don't see the point in lying. I'm not from Lobos. I'm from a long way away, and I honestly don't know what's going on. I've been to Lobos before but – and you don't have to believe this part if you don't want – it was in a different time.'

'Ha!' Pry said. 'Well you certainly sound like an alien.'

'I'm human, but I'm definitely not your enemy. I just know I've lost my mates. I mean, it's fine, the Doctor doesn't really need looking after—'

'The Doctor?' Mariya interrupted. 'Doctor who?'

'My friend. She's just called "the Doctor". She's sound as a pound, though. What?' Even in the dark, she clocked a loaded glance shared between Pry and Mariya.

'*She?* Nothing.'

Yaz knew she'd said something wrong. The earth shook again and she felt dust rain down on her hair. It wasn't as bad this time, and she managed to stay upright. If these were mineshafts, they didn't seem very secure. The vibrations grew stronger. It sounded like a pneumatic drill. She could also dimly hear voices.

It took her a moment to realise that she could *see* too. There was light up ahead.

'He's back!' someone called as Pry emerged into the light.

Yasmin looked around and saw the tunnel opened out into a vast underground chamber. It was all a bit makeshift, but it looked like some sort of camp. There were canvases and tents and scaffolds. Lamps hung from cables that were wrapped around the scaffolding. An electricity generator rumbled away.

Humans and loba – all in hardhats with torches – milled around, going about their duties. It was all very efficient-looking, like a beehive. Meaty smells filled the cavern and reminded Yaz that she hadn't eaten in hours.

'Father!' A girl about her age threw herself into Pry's arms. 'Don't you ever do that again! I was so worried.' She playfully slapped his arm. 'Getting captured by a routine patrol! How careless can you be?'

Pry held her tight. 'You should know I'm not that easy to cage.'

The girl was really quite stunning. She had Mariya's olive skin and long black hair but her father's fangs and piercing blue eyes. Just like her father, she had a silver stripe in her hair. 'Who's this?'

'Jaya, this is Yaz,' Mariya said. 'We're ... looking after her for now. Could you take a look at her knee, please?'

Yaz looked down and saw her left leg was covered in bright red blood *and* whatever she'd crawled through in the tunnels. It looked worse than she'd anticipated.

'Of course,' Jaya said. 'That must hurt a lot. Come with me.'

The chamber seemed to be some sort of junction with numerous tunnels leading off in different directions. 'Can we get some help?' a voice echoed down one of the passages.

'No rest for the wicked,' Mariya said. She and Pry ran to lend a hand.

'It's OK,' Jaya said to her. 'They'll sort it out. Come with me, we don't want that leg to get infected.'

'Wait!' Yaz stopped dead. She saw a group of loba dragging a very familiar shape on a trolley into the main cavern via one of the larger tunnels. It was on its side and covered in a tarpaulin, but there was only one thing it could be. 'Hey!' she shouted. 'Where did you get that?'

Everyone stopped and looked at her. 'Who's she?' said a young loba.

'Never mind that!' Yaz said. 'That's my spaceship!'

Pry pulled the canvas back to reveal the TARDIS.

By now, Ryan had an audience of about fifty monks gathered around him, hanging off his every word.

'... and that was when I was like, "Oi Termite Monster! Nibble on this!" And I just blast him with lightning from my hands like I'm Storm from off the X-Men, and it was sick, and the Termite Monster was like BOOM, and I was like, "How do you like me now?"'

'Praise be!' said the young monk. 'But, Lord Rasmin, what's a Termite?'

'Oh. You don't get them here? OK.' Ryan became aware of one of the hovering spheres looming over his head. 'What's that all about?'

Tempika jumped up. 'Oh. That's for me. Excuse me Lord Rasmin.' The Eye glided away and Tempika scurried to keep up with it.

That seemed weird. Tempika had been glued to his side all night. Why so skittish now? Ryan excused himself and went after him, pushing through the monks. Some groaned that the show was over.

Ryan followed Tempika out of the banquet hall into the quiet hallway. 'Wait, Tempika. What is it? Is it about Yaz? My friend?' He felt a little bad for banging on about his travels when Yaz was missing. If he could help her, he should.

The monk hesitated, tongue-tied.

'I erm ... command you tell me using my angelic authority.'

The poor guy looked pained. 'O Lord Rasmin, you test me.'

'I'm just worried about my friend. I have to know if you know something.'

Tempika looked around and then came closer, speaking under his breath. 'I risk my life by telling you this, my lord. I have a contact in the rebel camp. He provides me with vital information about their plots. I sent a message via the Eye before dinner about your friend and he has responded.'

'A spy?' Ryan said.

'Please, I beg you, keep your voice down, Lord Rasmin! There are those, within the Temple, who have ... sympathy for the blasphemous rebel scum. You never know who's listening.'

Ryan nodded. 'Walls have ears. Got it. So what you gonna do?'

Tempika again checked no one was eavesdropping. Behind them in the hall, the monks seemed much more interested in talking to Graham, who was taking it in turns to 'bless' them by waving his hands over their heads. 'The

Eye will lead me to my source and will tell me what he's learned.'

'Cool. Can I come?'

'No! I mean … no, Your Wondrousness.'

Ryan folded his arms defiantly. 'Well you either let me tag along or I'll wait about a minute and then follow you. So, like, up to you.'

Tempika sighed. Ryan had him over a barrel and he knew it. 'Oh, very well, if you absolutely must.' He looked left and right. 'This way. Quickly.' He opened a wooden door and slipped through.

Ryan ducked through after him, and found himself in a dark cupboard, pressed against Tempika. 'Bruv? Is this where you meet him?'

He heard Tempika tut. 'Here! Put this on!' He felt Tempika thrust robes into his arms. 'Half of the brethren will follow us otherwise.'

'Ah, got it.' Ryan realised the long grey robes were sort of a tribute to the Doctor's coat. He pulled the hood over his head and face. 'Ready.'

'Stay close to me.'

The pair slipped out of the cloakroom the same way they'd entered. The Eye still waited patiently for them; with Tempika back, it resumed its course. Tempika followed, darting along the hall with Ryan doing his best to keep up.

'I'm telling you!' Graham's voice boomed down the corridor. 'I'm just a normal bloke. I ain't sitting on no cloud! We just travel around helping people where we can!'

'Your humility is truly godly, Good Doctor,' replied Mykados, and Ryan chuckled as they fled into the night.

'We normally meet ...' Tempika began.

'And just where do you think you're going?' The Doctor dropped down through one of the open archways and into their path.

'Oh my days, I hate it when you do that,' Ryan said. 'We need to get you a little cat bell.'

'Sneaking away from your own feast in disguise? Terrible manners, Rasmin. Can I come too? Looks like fun!' She gave him a grin.

'Absolutely not!' Tempika looked like he might have a breakdown at any minute. 'Oh, this really is a step too far!'

'Tempika has a spy in the rebel camp,' Ryan explained. 'I'm gonna see if he knows where Yaz is.'

The Doctor nodded. 'Good thinking, that man, I like it. But I should come too. I want to meet these rebels. Sounds like they might have the right idea, actually.'

Tempika shook his head. 'If my source sees three of us, he won't reveal himself. He has a lot at stake.'

Ryan pointed back at the banquet hall. 'Also, Gra ... the Good Doctor, I mean ... I think he might need rescuing. Mykados is literally taking it to church in there. Got him blessing everyone.'

The Doctor sighed. 'Great. OK. Tempika, is it? Rasmin is the most trusted servant of the Good Doctor and if anything was to happen to him, he'd be heartbroken.'

Ryan felt a little warm glow in his chest.

'Of course, Good Nurse. He'll be quite safe.'

'Good. Come straight back here. We'll get Yaz back together.'

Ryan nodded. The Doctor trusted him not to do anything stupid but he'd had to earn that trust.

The Eye bleeped, reminding them it was waiting for their action.

'Quickly,' Tempika said. 'We must hurry.'

The Doctor gave Ryan's arm a squeeze, and he chased after Tempika.

Chapter 11

'What are you doing with that?' Yaz asked angrily. 'You can't just go around stealing people's time machines!'

The small crowd of rebels looked at her, fairly, like she was insane.

'That's … that's ours,' she added sheepishly.

Pry looked at her shrewdly. 'I think you have some explaining to do.'

'Well! I think *you* do,' Yaz replied. 'Why did you steal this?'

Pry chuckled and looked to the younger loba who'd wheeled it down. 'Well?'

'We … we thought it was a new weapon. Something the Temple had installed.'

'We thought we should dismantle it,' said another. Spending so much time in the hillside had left everyone grimy with dust and soot.

'Good luck with that,' Yaz said, although she didn't want to test the Doctor's claim that the TARDIS was indestructible. 'It's not a weapon, it's a ship. It's harmless.'

The air seemed to clear as Yaz and Pry silently reached stalemate. 'Take the weight off your leg.' Mariya steered her to one of the camp beds.

'Your turn,' Pry growled at her. 'Who are you? *Really?*'

Yaz shrugged. Her knee now throbbed with a dull pain. 'I'm a time traveller. Honestly.' Sometimes the only course of action is to tell the truth, no matter how ridiculous it sounds. 'We travel through space and time. Me and my friends came here once before … I assume it was in your past … Things were different.'

'Different how?' Jaya said.

Where to start? 'Well for one thing, loba weren't wearing those collars. There weren't terrifying floating balls ready to stun you unconscious. There was no mention of a temple being in charge.'

Pry and Mariya shared a knowing glance. 'The Temple has ruled Lobos for almost six hundred years.'

Yaz tried to stretch her leg out. It hurt. 'Then I guess six hundred years ago was the last time we were here. Listen. I don't know what's going on, but my friend – the Doctor – almost certainly will.'

'The Doctor?' Jaya asked.

'You said that before,' Pry said.

Jaya looked bewildered. 'The Good Doctor?'

'What?' Yaz said, now as confused as she was.

'The Good Doctor, it is said,' Jaya explained, 'came to Lobos six hundred years ago. The Temple built our whole society around him. He's a god.'

Yaz blinked. 'He? Oh, something has definitely got lost in translation here.'

The corridors shook again, the ground quaking under Yaz's feet. She gripped Jaya for support. Some of the scaffolding came loose, clanging to the floor. Debris rained down on them.

'Not being funny, but are we safe in here?'

Another surreptitious glance between Pry and Mariya said otherwise. Why were they down here anyway? Wouldn't it be more sensible to get as far away from the Temple as possible? 'Are these mines still … mined?'

'No. Not for a long time,' Mariya said, looking uncertainly at the ceiling.

'How's your knee?' Pry asked. 'Jaya, get her bandaged now. And find her some clean clothes, she reeks.'

'Thanks,' Yaz said. 'What do you expect? I just crawled through …'

Pry ignored her. 'We need to move on from this section. Everyone. Pack up. We're leaving in ten, unless you want to be buried alive.'

Everyone sprung to action, packing the camping stoves, cots, trestle tables and tools. 'Come over to the medical bay,' said Jaya, helping her up. 'Let's have a look at this knee.'

Yaz looked up at the stalactites overhead. She didn't fancy being underneath them if they all came crashing down.

The earth stirred again, like it was waking up.

'Good Doctor,' said one old monk, 'which is the greatest sin?'

'Good Doctor,' said another, 'can any sin be redeemed?'

'Good Doctor,' said a third, 'is thought alone as sinful as action?'

'OK!' said Graham, standing up. 'The Good Doctor wants a cup of tea – milk, two sugars – and to speak to the Good Nurse in private please. Um, like now.'

From where she was watching on the windowsill, the Doctor grinned, kicking her legs back and forth. It was all right for her – she was having a day off from being in charge.

Mykados stood and clapped his hands sharply. 'You heard him. Be gone! At once! You there, serving girl, fetch the Good Doctor whatever he desires.' Yianna bowed and hurried out of the room.

'You too, if that's all right, Mykados.' Graham couldn't keep up the act for a minute longer or he was going to pop.

'Of course, my supreme light, whatever you wish. Perhaps you might enjoy resting in my private reading room.'

'Thanks, mate.'

Mykados led Graham and the Doctor up a narrow winding staircase and along endless candlelit corridors until they came to a much more snug room – a cross between a library and an office, thought Graham. Shelves and shelves of dusty old books, with further volumes piled high on tables. Mykados bowed and left them alone.

Graham flopped down into an ostentatious armchair, massaging his temples. 'Tell you what, being a supreme light is chuffin' hard work.'

'Graham, you're doing an amazing job,' the Doctor said, popping her head out of the door to check the coast was clear. She seemed satisfied they could talk freely. 'While they're treating you like royalty, we're not in any trouble and they'll ask "how high" when we say "jump"!'

'Oh come on, I dunno how much longer I can keep this up for.'

'I know. But if you can, try until we get Yaz back, and then …'

'And then what?'

The Doctor perched on a footstool. 'Oh, Graham,' she sighed. 'I'm not liking what I'm seeing here. Are you?'

Graham shook his head. 'It's … it's mad! We was only here for a few hours and now we're a whole religion or something!'

'And not a very pleasant one if you're a woman or loba.' She threw her arms up, exasperated. 'There was some sort of an epidemic centuries ago. The Temple has very conveniently pinned it on both women and loba. Funny how that happens isn't it?' She sprung off her stool. Graham noted she only ever sat still for about two minutes at a time, she had the energy of a hummingbird. 'I can't even blame it on Mykados – although the jury's still out on him – look at these fusty old books. They go back hundreds of years. No one's even questioning them. It's just become the way it is. And tradition, for the sake of tradition, is one of my least favourite things in the whole world. Worse than olives.'

'What's wrong with olives?'

'We don't have time to go into what's wrong with them right now, Graham, we'd be here for weeks. We need to hope Ryan can find out where Yaz is.'

'What? Where's Ryan? Those two, honestly. Like herding kittens. Just when you think you know where they both are, one of them starts to wander off in a different direction.'

'Secret mission, but he's in safe hands, I promise. Well, I hope. Once we have Yaz back, I need to … fix things.' She strolled around the library, pausing at a tall, thin teak cabinet, padlocked shut. She turned the bronze lock over in her palm. 'Hmmm. Wonder what they keep in here? The really potent misogyny and racism maybe?'

'This ain't your fault.'

The Doctor, usually so daft, was suddenly very serious. She let the padlock clang against the cupboard. 'Isn't it?'

Graham looked up. The bottle-green glass lantern on the ceiling started to swing side to side before the whole room started to shake. The Doctor clutched a bookcase while Graham could only grip the arms of the chair. A couple of books clattered to the floor. As quickly as it had started, it settled.

'What was that?' Graham said, his heart racing. 'Earthquake?'

The Doctor frowned. 'I don't know. And I don't like not knowing.'

'Even less than olives?'

'Don't be silly, Graham. Olives are far worse.'

The taverna had barely changed at all in six centuries. It was small and cramped, but cosy, with jam-jar lanterns dangling from the ceiling. The clientele was a mixture of humans and loba, swinging tankards aloft and singing noisily. The air was thick with oaky tobacco smoke from the long pipes some of the patrons puffed on.

On a little stage in an alcove in the corner, an old silver-grey loba played what looked a bit like an accordion. Ryan didn't recognise the song, but it sounded like the sea shanties they used to do at school – 'What Shall We Do With The Drunken Sailor?' or something.

'I'd rather be, all out at sea,
sunk for the rest of me life.
I'd still feel better,
Down fifty foot wetter,
Than home with the kids and the wife!'

The bar – filled with sailors, fishermen and dockhands by the looks, and smell, of things – cheered raucously and raised their glasses. Ryan thought he'd probably quite like a wife and kids some day, but laughed and clapped along anyway.

'Don't draw attention to us,' Tempika hissed. They'd dumped their robes outside. Without his cowl, Tempika just looked like a regular guy, about Ryan's age. 'The tavern is a mixed place, but I doubt we'd be very welcome here if they knew we were from the Temple. I mean, my goodness, imagine if they knew Lord Rasmin walked among them. There'd be a riot.'

'Mate, chill! It's fine!' Ryan adopted the same 'I definitely belong in here' stance he used at student union bars in Sheffield. 'Who are we looking for?'

'Over there … don't make it obvious, Lord Rasmin! In the corner.'

Ryan twisted around, almost swiping a whole barrel of drinks over. 'Sorry!' he said. Dyspraxic people as tall as him didn't really *do* discreet. He saw a lone figure drinking in the corner booth, bathed in shadows, scribbling something intently into some sort of journal by the looks of things.

'I need to take him a tankard.' Tempika waited his turn at the heaving bar and bought three pints of the same foamy, fruity ale Ryan had sampled earlier. Six hundred years earlier, but also that day. Oh man, jetlag was gonna catch up with him any minute now.

Tempika carried the ale over on a tray. Ryan hung back, not wanting to scare the source away. In the feeble candlelight, Ryan saw the spy wore a khaki scarf wrapped all around his head. Only piercing blue eyes peered out through the gloom. From the huge furry paws and sharp claws, Ryan saw he was loba.

'Who's this?' the loba growled.

'No one,' Tempika said, sliding into the booth. Ryan squeezed himself in next to him. 'A friend.'

'Do you trust him?'

'With my life,' Tempika nodded earnestly.

'Good enough for me. Now give me my drink and my gold, naked ape.'

Tempika handed over the tankard and a little pocket of jangling coins. 'There you go. Now tell us: where are the rebels?'

'And is there a human girl with them?' Ryan added urgently.

'The rebels continue to excavate the caves in the hillside. But the land is becoming unstable. Pry's moving the entire group to the old tin mines to the east of Old Town.'

'Is that what the earthquakes are about?' Ryan asked. There'd been a pretty bad tremor as they'd driven to the taverna.

'Indeed.'

'It's madness,' Tempika said. 'They'll destroy all of Old Town if they're not careful.' He turned to Ryan. 'Already there's been landslides. Huge cracks, splitting houses in two.'

'All to destroy the Temple,' the mysterious loba hissed.

'What about my friend?' Ryan asked.

'She is with the rebels.'

'Oh, amazing!' Ryan felt his shoulder unclench, although then wondered if she was still with them *voluntarily*. 'Where with the rebels? And is she safe?'

'I cannot vouch for her safety. By now they'll be in the East Mines.'

'All of them?' Tempika said. 'You're sure?'

'All of them. And their weapons and drills.'

Tempika smiled. 'This is it. We can bring an end to all this. No more attacks, no more violence. This could all end tonight. Without Pry, they're nothing.'

'What?' Ryan said.

'Quickly! We must inform Mykados!' Tempika jumped out of the booth, but not before the strange old loba slipped him a sheet of paper from the journal. Tempika tucked it into his waistband.

'Wait!' said Ryan. 'What about Yaz?'

'We can retrieve her *and* stop the rebellion! We know where they're going! Come now! We must return to the Temple.'

Ryan looked back at the hooded loba. He swore he saw just a hint of a smile in those cunning eyes. With a bad feeling in his gut, he picked an awkward path after Tempika.

Chapter 12

The Mayor of Old Town, Bemus Belen, lived in a heavily guarded villa on a promontory overlooking the sea. Mykados's buggy slowed to a halt before the grand gates, and a guard checked inside the cart before waving him and his escort into the compound.

As he did every night, Mykados came to the villa to bless Belen, his wife and daughters. It had been this way for generations, tradition, although Mykados found their nightly visits to be … fruitful.

The loba butler, Rex, a grizzled, grey, frail old dog who'd served under the last three mayors, welcomed him into the palatial home and led him upstairs to Belen's private office. With the windows open, the drapes billowed in the sea breeze. Mykados found the home tasteless, lavish. If it was up to him, only the Temple would be allowed gold and jewels to exalt the Good Doctor. The villa felt gaudy and inappropriate.

Rex tapped on the office doors before entering. Mykados glimpsed the Mayor very swiftly back away from the loba serving girl who'd brought him a tray of cheese and wine.

Mykados said nothing, but stored the detail away for use when it was time for a different mayor.

'Your Grace, please come on in!' Belen boomed, red-faced. He was a large, gregarious man with olive skin and oily black hair. 'Leave us,' he told the serving girl and she scurried past Mykados, head down.

'Let us pray, Mayor Belen.'

One wall of his office housed a candlelit shrine: a bronze statue of the Good Doctor in a tiled alcove. Belen knelt on the red stool before it. 'Thank you for leaving the feast, Your Grace.'

'Not at all.' Mykados blessed Belen, making the square of Tordos on his forehead.

'People are talking, Mykados,' Belen said, his eyes closed. 'People are saying He has returned.'

Word travelled dangerously fast in Old Town. Mykados had hoped to keep Belen in the dark a little longer. The buffoon would only interfere. 'A man has arrived on Lobos.'

'Is it Him?'

Mykados so badly wanted to believe it was. The Book of Truths said it would happen. How else could it be that a man so closely resembled the sole image kept in the most secure vault in the Temple? But his gut told him that on the day the Good Doctor returned, he would feel more certain in his heart. As certain as his love and devotion. The man presently waiting for him back at the Temple ... did not inspire that. Mykados had never in his entire life *doubted* the Good Doctor ... and yet ...

He smiled at Belen. 'I believe he could be.'

'He *could* be?' Belen's eyes snapped open. 'Your Grace? Are you saying that a *god* walks among us?'

Mykados poured a glass of wine from the tankard and blessed it before handing it to the Mayor. 'You seem worried, Bemus? Was this day not foretold?'

Belen stuttered. 'Well, yes ... I mean ... I just mean ... well what *does* this mean? The Book of Truths teaches us He would only return at the End of Days to take us with Him to—'

'Yes, Belen, I know the scripture.' Mykados placed a hand on the Mayor's head. 'Do not hold fear in your heart and trust in the Good Doctor. If He has returned, it must be to save us. It is a sign that this war with the rebels is drawing to a close.'

The Mayor looked up at him. 'Do you think so?'

'Bemus. Do you trust in the Good Doctor?'

'With all my heart.'

'Then trust in me.' Mykados patted the Mayor's shoulder. 'I have faith that this visitation is a sign. The Good Doctor is here to help us destroy the rebellion. Do you give me power to act in the best interest of the people of Old Town?'

'Yes ... Do what you think you must.'

Mykados bowed his head, hiding a slight smile. 'Bless you, my child.'

Yaz tried to walk on her now bandaged leg. Jaya had cleaned her up and rubbed some sort of anaesthetic cream on it, a foul-smelling, eggy concoction. At first it had felt stingy, then warm and now sort of numb. It was fine, she could walk on it, albeit with a slight limp.

On the other side of the cavern, she saw Pry inspecting the TARDIS, tracing the door with his paws.

'You won't get in,' Yaz told him. 'Where did Jaya go?'

'To fetch supplies,' Pry said sharply. 'This is a box. A wooden box.'

Yaz smiled and shook her head. 'It's so much more than that.'

Pry's eyes narrowed. 'Oh, I know. It's a symbol of death on Lobos. Do you have any idea how many loba died building that monstrosity on the hill?'

Yaz said nothing. What was there to say? She couldn't even pretend to be surprised. History, wherever she went it seemed, was built on the bones of slavery.

'This is a time machine, you say?'

'Yes.'

'Can you operate it?'

'No,' said Yaz. She'd watched the Doctor closely and knew what some of the buttons did, but it always seemed like the TARDIS and the Doctor worked together as partners, not user and machine.

'But,' said Pry, 'this thing could, in theory, take me back in time?'

Oh, she saw where this was heading. 'In *theory*, yes.'

He seemed to sniff the TARDIS. 'I could go back. I could destroy the Temple before they even started it. I could free Lobos before it was enslaved.'

'Pry, no …' Yaz told him as sympathetically as she could. 'What's done is done, you can't rewrite history.'

'Why not?' he snarled. 'You said it yourself: the Temple has done just that.'

'This is different. You're talking … paradoxes.' The Doctor had tried to explain this to her numerous times, but every time it eventually turned her brain to mush. 'Pry, you only exist because history ran the way it did. If you go back into your own timeline, you risk changing the events that brought about your birth. Mariya's birth. Jaya's birth.'

'Perhaps a necessary sacrifice.'

Yaz shook her head slowly. For the first time, she didn't feel wholly safe with Pry. There was an intensity in his eyes. She'd seen it before: *obsession.* 'You don't mean that, Pry. I mean, how would you even do it? How do you stop a *religion*?'

He considered this for a moment. 'You kill god.'

When cloister bells rang out, Graham had learned, nothing good was about to happen. When they'd started chiming, the Doctor tossed aside the Book of Truths she'd been reading, and tutting at, for the last hour, and fled the reading room. All he could do was jog to keep up with her. This had better be good for his heart. 'Doctor, will you slow down!' he panted.

'One day, not today.' She pointed at the steady procession of monks and Temple guards. 'They're all heading towards the chapel. C'mon slowpoke, let's see what's happening.'

Sure enough, it seemed the cloister bells were some sort of call to prayer. They got louder and louder as they approached the chapel. The Brethren dutifully filed into the grand church. All the Doctor and Graham had to do was blend into the crowd.

'Halt!' commanded one old monk. 'No womenfolk allowed in the Temple!'

The Doctor slowly turned on her heel. 'He said it was OK!' She pointed at Graham. 'Don't mess with the Good Doctor!'

'New rules!' Graham added. 'We like womenfolk now, keep up.'

The monk looked very confused but allowed them to pass. They descended wide stairs that led into the hall through a side door. Graham realised the entire Temple was a rabbit warren of corridors and tunnels, but they all led to his shrine. Efficiently, monks filled the front pews and guards the back. The Doctor pulled her hood over her hair, the only woman in the entire chapel.

'Look!' she announced, taking hold of his hand. 'There's Ryan!'

Ryan hovered uneasily at the front near the altar. The Doctor cut through the crowd to reach him.

'Ryan!' she hissed.

'Oh mate, this is so mad,' he said on seeing them, shifting nervously from foot to foot.

'What's going on?' the Doctor said. 'Are you OK? Is Yaz OK?'

'I'm not sure *anything* is OK. When we got back, Tempika went off to tell Mykados about the meeting and then that bell started ringing. I dunno what's going on.'

'But do you know where Yaz is?' Graham added.

'She's with the rebels. There was this weird loba bloke, this spy, and he says she's OK.'

'As their prisoner?'

'I don't think so … I think she escaped from jail and went with them.'

'I don't know why I worry so much about you all when you're all so brilliant,' the Doctor said. 'Oh, here we go.'

Mykados took to his pulpit, flanked by Tempika and a serious-looking man in a blue guard's uniform. Graham guessed he was in charge. 'Good Doctor, Good Nurse, Lord Rasmin and cherished brethren, I bear excellent tidings.'

A hush fell over the whole chapel.

'Brother Tempika has discovered that the dangerous terrorists who threaten peace and stability on Lobos have been traced to the East Mines. They cower like cockroaches in the darkness.'

A murmur ran through the pews.

'Brothers, hush. After decades of unrest, of violence and murder, we have an opportunity to end the insurgence and restore peace. I have consulted with Captain Makris, and we shall despatch all troops to Kanda to intercept the rebels should they try to escape above ground. Brothers, quite simply, there is nowhere left for Pry and his traitors to run or hide.' Mykados looked to Graham. 'It is very clear to me, Your Almighty Goodness, that your return foresaw this holy victory. On this, the eve of Doctor's Day, we shall *destroy* the rebellion. It is a sign!'

Graham looked to the Doctor. She fixed him with her gravest look and he just hoped she had a plan.

Battle-worn helicopters took off from a helipad at the very top of Old Town. Ryan couldn't get his head around Lobos: sometimes it felt like the olden days on Earth, until you saw the floating drones and choppers. He guessed any wealth this world had was being redirected into the church or the military. At the same time as the helicopters lifted off, armoured dune buggies – bigger, sturdier and deadlier than the ones the monks used – bounced off over the rough terrain towards Kanda.

'We're coming too,' the Doctor told Mykados. The four of them stood on the helipad on the very top of the cliffs, overlooking the entire coastline.

'Oh my goodness, no. I insist you remain at the Temple. It isn't safe. The terrorists will resist, there's no doubt of that.'

'Good Doctor …?' she prompted Graham.

'Yeah. I order you take us to the East Mines. No harm must … erm … befall our beloved, heavenly … pal.'

Mykados frowned. 'But … my Lord, are you not … all-powerful? Surely she is impervious to injury?'

Ryan looked from the Doctor to Graham. OK, this god lie was starting to wear a bit thin. And Ryan suspected Mykados was starting to think so too – his gushing was getting noticeably less … gushing.

'When we move amongst mankind, we are no different to you, trapped by the earthly physical constraints of this primitive realm,' said the Doctor with gusto. 'After all, is it not said, you were made in our image?'

'That's why, if something was to happen to Yaz, I'd be greatly … miffed.' Graham folded his arms and tried to look butch. It really didn't work.

This seemed to convince the priest. 'Ah, very well.' He signalled to a guard. 'Sergeant Barlos, please escort the

Good Doctor and his apostles to the East Mines at Kanda. I'll ride with Captain Makris and meet you there. I don't need to tell you how precious your cargo is.'

'Of course, Your Grace.' Barlos was another black guy almost as tall as Ryan but twice as buff. 'It's this way.'

Unable to look them in the eye, Barlos led them to one of the armoured buggies, all the while the Doctor muttering something about warfare and bloodshed. The Doctor hopped into the back of the buggy, more like a tank really, and then offered Ryan and Graham a hand up. With Barlos in the driver's seat, they set off into arid wasteland. From what Ryan remembered, there was a township between Old Town and Kanda, but it was long gone now, replaced with rubble and ruins.

'What's the plan, Doctor?' asked Graham. 'Please say this is one of the times you have an actual plan and not just the illusion that you have a plan?'

'How dare you,' the Doctor said huffily. 'There's *always* a plan, even if the plan is *pretending* I have a plan.' The Doctor grinned. 'But yes, there is a plan. It's very simple. Get Yaz out of those mines before some numpty starts firing.'

Ryan liked that plan.

It was only a short drive to the East Mines, and Ryan was glad of it because he hadn't taken his travel sickness pills and the ride was mad bumpy. In the distance something like coyotes or wolves howled at the moons. Or perhaps it was just something the loba did, who knew?

Kicking up a cloud of orange dust, the buggy swerved down a dirt track into a quarry. There was a rusty mineshaft and some abandoned mining equipment, but it looked like this hadn't been a working pit for some time.

Barlos brought the buggy to a halt alongside the one in which Mykados and his senior monks waited. 'Wait here, please, Your Goodness. You should be safe here.'

'Should?' Ryan asked.

'Shhh,' the Doctor said, deep in thought.

The helicopters circled overhead, their spotlights sweeping across the rocky terrain. The Temple guards formed a barrier at the two entrances to the mine – one a lift shaft and the other a cave mouth with old tracks for mine carts. Captain Makris ordered his men into position, weapons trained on the exits, and then returned to where the buggies were stationed. Makris was a tall, leathery man, with silver hair and a white scar cutting through his left eyebrow.

'Progress report, captain?' Mykados commanded.

'Troops have every exit guarded. Your Grace, the rebels have no way out.'

Far below the surface, Yaz struggled to keep up with Mariya as they moved through the tunnels. The anaesthetic seemed to be wearing off; her knee hummed with pain. She now wore thick combat pants and a khaki T-shirt – supplied by Mariya – and felt very Che Guevara. Or at least, she might if she weren't limping quite so much.

They moved in a steady convoy. Almost everybody else carried weapons and equipment, pulling trolleys and carts behind them. At the head of the line, a human member of the resistance drove what Pry called the excavator. It looked about the size of a forklift truck but had a sealed cockpit and a wicked-looking corkscrew attached to the front. It looked like it had seen better days, it was filthy and covered in rust and duct tape. It chugged through the tunnels, churning out choking exhaust fumes.

'What's that for?' Yaz asked.

'The excavator?' Mariya replied, not stopping. 'We stole it and fixed it up. It's a simple plan, Yasmin. We're going to bring down the Temple. And I mean that literally. Old Town is already unstable. Has been for generations. The hillside was irresponsibly mined. They should have built their stupid great Temple somewhere more sound, but they didn't.'

'You're going to cause a cave-in?'

'Yes. Oh don't worry. We expect they'll have plenty of time to evacuate Old Town, it's more symbolic.'

We expect wasn't good enough. 'Symbolic of what?'

'The fall of the Temple. Yaz, there are pockets of resistance all over Lobos. We have people in Kanda, Skizip, Famatown, and in the mountains to the north. The Temple is entirely based in Old Town, but their control spreads across Lobos. If we can bring down that … figurehead … it means we've won. Humans and loba all over the world will see that the Temple is *weak*. Collapsed. Finished. And a new age will begin.'

The earth jolted like a bucking bronco, and Yaz fell on top of Mariya. At least this time she had a soft landing. This was no mere tremor, though. The earth seemed to roar. Chunks of rock crumbled. Yaz held her breath as Mariya covered her head with a protective arm. 'Mariya?'

'This is a bad one,' she whispered. 'Hold on.'

She was going to be buried alive and there was nothing she could do about it. Yaz clamped her teeth together, screwed her eyes shut and waited for a world of pain …

And then, once again, it stopped.

She counted to about five in her head before she dared to breathe again.

'Quickly!' Pry hollered from up ahead in the tunnel. 'Move! Move! Move! This section isn't safe.'

Mariya picked herself up. 'It's fine,' she said. 'This happens sometimes. We mine an area to weaken it, and then we move on. It's fine,' she said again.

Yaz wasn't convinced at all.

Graham watched as a party of Temple guards spilled from the tunnel's mouth, guns raised.

'Report,' Makris commanded into his radio.

'Nothing, sir.' A response crackled. 'No signs of life. Over.'

'Have they been here?'

'Inconclusive. Over.'

'What about the Eyes? Are they seeing anything further down?'

'Negative, sir.'

Next to Makris, Mykados looked furious. 'Where is Tempika? Bring him to me,' he ordered angrily.

The Temple guards scattered, searching for Tempika. 'We can't find him, Your Grace,' they reported. 'He must have remained at the Temple.'

'In the name of the Doctor! That feckless boy will be the death of me!'

Ryan stepped up. 'I was with him at the tavern. The bloke said they were moving to the East Mines, I swear.'

Makris stood to attention. 'Your Grace. We can either storm the mines – we'll have them outnumbered – or we can collapse this exit, block their escape. This will divert them back towards Old Town where we can intercept them.'

'Or bury them alive!' The Doctor stepped between Mykados and Makris. 'You can't collapse the mine, you'll kill them.'

'Who is this woman?' Makris said with thinly veiled disgust.

'I am sorry, Good Nurse,' Mykados said earnestly. 'But this bloody conflict, as you know, has played out for many long years. These terrorists … they stand against everything the Good Doctor has taught us. They would deny His glory. If we can bring the rebellion to an end, we must. It's a handful of insurgents, no more.'

'No! Not like this! There can be no justification for this – least of all him!' She pointed at Graham.

Sheepishly Graham stepped forward. 'Well, you heard her. There's people down there! Our friend is down there!'

The guards and monks looked uneasily between Graham and Mykados.

'Graham,' the Doctor breathed, grasping his shoulders. 'They won't listen to me. It has to be you.'

'I can't …'

'You absolutely *can*.'

'OK. Here goes nothing …' Graham climbed up onto a great sandstone boulder, looking down over the entire mine. He took a deep breath. 'Erm, listen up! Oi! You lot! Are you listening?' The guards and monks stopped what they were doing and looked around to witness their savour. Graham nervously continued his sermon. 'Now I don't know what people have been saying about me, but I think … I think you got it wrong. I think people on Lobos have been adding little bits and taking bits away.'

Below the monks, in particular, turned to one another in alarm. What he'd just said was … blasphemy. Their god had just blasphemed.

Subtly, the Doctor slipped her sonic screwdriver out of her inside pocket and held it up to the air.

'What you doing?' Ryan asked.

'It's time for the floor show. Watch this,' the Doctor muttered.

Graham cleared his throat. 'Look. I'm pretty sure I never told you it was OK to go about killing people because they don't think the same as you. I never said that, did I?

Once again, the brothers looked to one another, chattering amongst themselves.

Mykados's nostrils flared. 'The Book of Truths is infallible!' he shouted. 'Those who strayed from the Word of the Good Doctor brought about the fall of civilisation. The Truth is the Righteous Path!'

'The Word, the Truth, the Path! What you on about, mate? It don't mean nothing if you ain't being *kind*!'

The air around Graham started to glow. Green, blue, gold, pink, purple. Ryan's mouth fell open. It was like that … aurora! The Northern Lights!

'What … how?'

The Doctor grinned.

'I bet that's in your book, right?' Graham continued. 'Love thy neighbour and all that? Do to others as you'd have done to you … erm … thou shall not … kill people? It's pretty obvious ain't it?'

The shimmering lights continued to swirl around Graham, growing even more intense. Some monks and troops cowered away in awe.

'Just be *nice*! I'm pretty sure that's what I said. Be nice! Killing people, burying them alive! Ain't very nice, is it?'

The lights died down.

'How'd you do that?' Ryan asked the Doctor.

The Doctor smiled. 'Easy-peasy. Some residual mine gases are still seeping up through the earth. Just burned them off at high temperatures to make some pretty colours! Looked nice, though, didn't it? Colours are lovely!'

You can't argue with that, thought Ryan.

'Enough!' Mykados roared. 'How many people have died at the hands of these murderers?'

'How many people have died by your guns?' Ryan shouted over him.

'Just stop!' Graham shouted. 'Um. He who lives by the sword, dies by the sword?'

'No! It ends now.' Mykados turned to Makris. 'Destroy the mine.'

'What?' No!' cried the Doctor. 'Please, Mykados. Don't do this. I'm begging you.'

Mykados drew himself tall. 'I don't take requests from women, least of all beggars.'

Uh-oh. The penny dropped for Ryan. This Mykados guy. He didn't believe them any more, if he ever really had done.

The High Priest swept past the Doctor and climbed onto the boulder alongside Graham. 'Brethren. How readily we accepted this man as the Good Doctor. What if this is witchcraft? Trickery? How can we trust what he says is the Truth?'

The troops and monks whispered among themselves. A bold young monk stepped forward. 'You saw him!' he yelled up. 'He can glow!'

'Phantasmagoria! This is not the first time Lobos has been visited by devils from the sky, by false prophets. Why would the Good Doctor preach mercy against violent heretics? Why? It is madness. It stands against His teachings.'

The Doctor looked up at Graham and gently shook her head. 'I am!' he said, giving it one last try. 'I am the Good Doctor and I command you to stop! We can end this peacefully.'

'These rebel heathens deny your grace. Why would you defend them so?'

'I ... I'm not,' said Graham. 'It's just ...'

'Just nothing!' Mykados grew angrier by the second. 'There can be no peace while the rebellion lives. We here have lost fathers, mothers, brothers and sisters to this reign of terror!' Spit sprayed from his lips. 'The Good Doctor would never ask this of the faithful.'

'Hear, hear!' one stocky soldier yelled. 'Destroy them!'

'No!' The Doctor shouted back.

Mykados's eyes narrowed, glaring up at Graham. 'I name thee charlatan. Tonight it ends!'

The crowd began to cheer. Graham could only look on in horror.

'Captain Makris. Destroy this mineshaft.'

'Yes, Your Grace. Unit B! Arm the explosives!'

'No!' The Doctor shouted, racing towards Makris. 'Stop! Our friend is down there!'

'Restrain them!' Mykados ordered.

Troops moved in and grasped the Doctor.

'Oi! Let her go!' Ryan went to help her, but he too was held back.

Makris's radio crackled. 'The device is in position, Captain.'

'Affirmative. Get to a safe distance.'

'Aye, Captain.'

Ryan struggled against the monk who was pinning his arms down. 'Get off me!' Only then he felt warm breath on his ear. 'Lord Rasmin,' said a familiar voice. 'If you want to help your friends, come with me, don't ask questions.' It was Tempika. Ryan swivelled around and saw he had his hood pulled all the way down over his face.

'What?'

'I can't explain ... but come! Now! While everyone's distracted.'

Ryan surveyed the chaotic scene. Now both troops and monks were racing to get themselves in position. Graham – bless him – he'd tried, but failed.

The Doctor twisted back to glower up at Mykados. 'Mykados! This is cold-blooded murder! What does it say about that in your precious books?'

'The cause is just, and not one among us is without sin, woman. Captain? Are we ready?'

'Yes, Your Grace.'

'Do it.'

'Unit B. Proceed.'

'OK,' Ryan said to Tempika. 'Let's go.'

The convoy continued deeper and deeper into the heart of the mines. 'Keep going!' Pry called back. 'We're almost there.'

Yaz was exhausted. Her knee ached and her boots were rubbing blisters on her heels. She had to keep going. She had to find the others.

The earth started to quake again.

And this time it didn't stop.

'What's happening?' she hissed to Jaya by her side. A deep rumble, as deep as thunder, grew louder and louder.

Jaya said nothing, but her eyes glowed in the dark. And they looked scared.

'Jaya?' Yaz clung to her. 'What *is* that?'

It sounded *big*.

The blast was deafening.

Graham covered his ears. The earth under his feet shook and grumbled. He fell to his knees, clinging to the boulder.

A vast mushroom cloud billowed up from out of the earth, clogging the air with thick black dust. Through the fog, he watched as the old mineshaft wavered for a second before its long legs snapped and caved in on themselves. The old cage plummeted down the shaft with an almighty clang as it ricocheted against the sides.

'Doctor?' Graham called down to her.

The Doctor looked up at him in horror, lips parted, eyes wide.

'Report, Captain Makris?' Mykados said.

'The device was detonated successfully, Your Grace. We have collapsed the East Mine.'

Mykados closed his eyes like his was thanking his saints. 'Excellent. Praise be.'

Chapter 13

Under armed guard, the Doctor and Graham were driven back to Old Town and then frogmarched into the Temple. As they walked over the bridge in a convoy of monks and Temple guards, Graham could sense sadness coming off the Doctor in powerful waves but said nothing. What could he possibly say? Lovely, sweet, young Yasmin. What would they tell her family? He blinked back tears.

Dawn had broken. Two beautiful sunrises popped out of the sea, like a pair of pink grapefruits, but Graham didn't even see them. All he could think about was Yaz.

'I want him found,' Mykados said. 'How could he just vanish?'

'He's an angel!' the Doctor shouted. 'Maybe he sprouted wings and flew away!'

Makris and Mykados turned around and glared at her. She glared right back.

'Yeah,' Graham whispered to her. 'But where is he, really?'

'I have no idea,' the Doctor said through her teeth. 'He was there one minute and gone the next. Maybe he really did vanish into thin air.'

They were, of course, talking about Ryan. On one hand, he'd get a clip round the earhole for wandering off, but on the other Graham hoped his step-grandson was working on getting them out of this fix.

They were steered back into the Temple and marched all the way back to Mykados's reading room. 'Guard the door please,' Mykados told one of the Temple guards. 'But wait outside.'

The guard nodded and closed the door behind himself, leaving them alone with Mykados. The Doctor slumped down in the armchair, looking like a surly teenager. 'Go on, then,' she said. 'Let's get it over with.'

Graham hung back in the corner of the library, quite happy to let the Doctor be the Doctor once more.

'Get what over with?' Mykados asked.

'The inevitable interrogation. Who are we? Where have we come from? What do we want? But given that you just dropped a mineshaft on my best friend's head, I'm not feeling especially cooperative, it must be said.'

Mykados walked slowly around the grand desk and sat in his creaky chair. The reading room smelled of incense and centuries old paper. It took Graham all the way back to Sunday School in Chingford when he was a little boy. 'If your friend is as celestial as you claim, she'll be perfectly safe, won't she?'

The Doctor didn't take her eyes off Mykados. 'Oh, I hope for your sake that's true.'

'Is that a threat?'

'Yes. You'll wish I was a myth.'

'I knew it. You're charlatans, the lot of you! I wouldn't be surprised if this is some nonsense Pry and his cronies concocted.'

The Doctor smiled. 'Oh no, that's the plot twist! You're *almost* right! We did come to Lobos before, and I suppose we did save the world. All true! The Temple has just either got some parts mixed up or, worst-case scenario, wilfully manipulated them to spread propaganda.'

'Oh really?' Mykados said making a steeple with his fingers under his pointed chin. 'And, pray tell, which parts did we get wrong in your humble opinion?'

'Well, for one thing,' the Doctor said with a broad smile, '*I'm* the Good Doctor. How do you do?'

Yaz followed Jaya and Mariya into a new cavern. 'I'm confused,' she said. 'What was that explosion? Was that you?'

The rebels spilled into a large, startlingly beautiful, cave with shards of natural light piercing through from the surface above. At the centre of the cave was a tranquil underground lake. The surface shone like a black mirror.

'This is the site we were thinking of, what do you think?' a young loba told Pry.

Pry surveyed the cave and nodded. 'Yes, this is perfect. Everyone! Set up camp. We'll be here until the final phase begins. Good work,' he told the younger loba.

'Well?' Yaz stepped under Pry's nose and waited for an answer. '*Was* it you?'

Pry smiled properly for the first time since she'd met him. 'Yes *and* no …'

There was a scuffle from the far side of the cavern as two men climbed down through a crevice. Yaz swung her torch upwards and realised she recognised one of the silhouettes. 'Ryan?' She ran around the edge of the lake and met them as they reached her level.

'There she is!' Ryan beamed.

Yaz almost threw her arms around him, but settled for a fist-bump. They were often split up and reunited, but it didn't get any less reassuring as time went on. 'You all right? Where's the Doctor? And Graham?'

Ryan looked up to the surface. 'They're OK. I think. Oh I dunno, it's messed up. They all think Graham's a god.'

How long had she been down these mines? Was she hearing things? 'What?'

Jaya barged past her shoulder to get to Ryan's companion. He wore a monk's habit, which he now pulled off as Jaya gave him a lingering kiss. 'I'm so glad you're safe,' she said before turning to Ryan with a mischievous grin. 'Nice to see you again.'

'Again?' Ryan said.

'We met in the tavern earlier.'

'Eh? That was you?'

'A disguise! Big furry gloves! Head scarf!' Jaya growled in the same deep voice she'd used early. It was uncanny to hear it coming from such a petite girl.

'I thought you were a big hairy male!'

The monk smiled. 'Careful, Lord Rasmin, that's my future wife you're talking about ...'

'Mate, you can call me Ryan now. This is my friend, Yaz. Yaz this is Brother Tempika.'

'Please. Just Tempika.'

'Lord Rasmin? What? Ryan, what have I missed?' Yaz said.

'I can explain everything!' Pry shouted over. 'But get the man a drink first. He's risked his neck for us more times than I can count.'

As the rebels unloaded their packs and settled into their new camp, the lake water was purified and ready for drinking. Yaz gulped it down, her throat so tense it hurt. It felt like she'd been running for hours. Sometimes it felt like she hadn't stopped running since she met the Doctor.

Mariya lit a camping stove and cooked some rations. The little family, Yaz and Ryan gathered around her fire until it was ready. If the earth didn't keep shuddering and they weren't a million feet underground, it could be like Girl Guides, Yaz mused. Mariya shared around the rations in metal tins, some sort of chewy meat that reminded Yaz a little of duck.

'It worked,' Tempika relayed, recounting his chapter of the story through mouthfuls of food. 'They believed the intel I gave them.'

'They collapsed the East Mine.' Pry nodded thoughtfully, seemingly considering what this meant for them.

'Is that the blast we felt?' Yaz asked.

'Yes!' Jaya replied. 'But, of course, I'd told Tempika where we were *really* going: the Caves of Hezos.'

'When you slipped him that note!' Ryan said.

'Yes. It's not the first time someone from the Temple insisted they come with me when I meet my *informant*.' Tempika held Jaya's hand. 'So we have a system. If someone else is present, she tells me the misinformation and then finds a way to relay the real movements of the resistance – all coded of course, just in case.'

'How did you hack the Eye?' Ryan asked.

Jaya smiled. 'Oh we have Dayna.' She waved at a young loba girl on the other side of the cavern. 'Dayna is very clever, and those Eyes are getting old now, they're easy to hack. We just have to be careful no one else at the Temple tries to interact with them …'

Mariya served Ryan his rations. 'We've suspected for a while the Temple are becoming wary of a possible mole within their ranks. It was time to pull Tempika out. They'd execute him if he was discovered. He's been leading Mykados on a merry little dance for months now.'

Tempika looked a little sad. 'You know, all I ever wanted was to join the brotherhood. My father joined up, so did my brothers. But once I learned of the brutality the brotherhood use against the loba, against rebels, against women, I was sickened. It started as doubt, and then confusion, and then total disenchantment. Not in the Good Doctor, you understand, just in the way the Temple is run. It simply isn't right.'

'I'm confused about one thing,' Yaz said. 'Why go to all that effort to lead them to believe you're in the East Mine?'

'If they think we're all dead it buys us some time for one thing,' Pry told her. 'But what those fools have just done is speed up our progress by *months*. We have one excavator and we have explosives, but – unfortunately – not ones we can detonate remotely. The idiots. They're so keen to see us all dead that they just made the hillside even less stable.'

'The earthquakes?' Ryan said.

'Our friends here are trying to bring down the Temple,' Yaz told him, hoping he'd pick up on her tone. 'Literally.' His brow furrowed slightly, which told her that he understood. Resistance or not, this was a terrible idea. But how to let them know that without getting shot or something?

'You're causing earthquakes?' Ryan looked from Pry to Mariya. 'People are gonna get hurt.'

'No!' Jaya insisted, brushing it off. 'There's already talk of evacuating Old Town.'

Tempika cleared his throat. 'But some of the brethren are saying they'll never abandon the Temple. That the earthquakes are a test of their faith.'

Pry let his empty ration dish clatter to the floor. 'I'm not responsible for their bloody-mindedness or their stupidity. Let them stay. Let them die on an altar of their prejudice.' He stood and went back to setting up the camp.

'And they really think your grandfather is the Good Doctor?' Jaya asked.

'He's not my ...' Ryan started. 'Oh never mind. Yeah. Well they did. I think it's all starting to unravel.'

'If Graham's a god ... what are we?' Yaz said.

'Angels.'

'Amazing.'

'It was for about an hour. But we're rumbled.'

Yaz turned to Tempika. 'Are they in trouble? What will this Mykados guy do if he finds out we're just well ... we're no angels?'

Tempika and Jaya shared a highly loaded glance. 'Mykados is fiercely devout. Dangerously. That's why ...'

'Go on,' Yaz prompted him.

'I was raised in the Temple,' Tempika said. 'My mother died in childbirth and I was raised by the sisters and then followed my father and brothers into the brethren when I was twelve. The first High Priest I served under was very, very old and when he died, Mykados took over ...'

'And?' Yaz asked.

'And things changed. Drop by drop, month by month, he introduced new rules and harsher punishments for violating the laws in the Book of Truths. Some of the brothers welcome the new direction, but then he reintroduced the executions, the stonings. Deep in my belly, I knew it was wrong. So, when I met Jaya, I felt it was a sign – her coming into my life – and I started feeding her information.'

Yaz was starting to like this guy. 'So how did you two meet?'

There was no mistaking the loving looks Jaya and Tempika were sharing. 'Picture this!' Jaya smiled. 'It was a sweltering solstice afternoon in Old Town. Market day. Everyone loves market day. All the fruit farmers from the flatlands at Famatown bring big trucks of ousfruit, gingy berries and rampas. Because I – more or less – pass as human, I went to ... *acquire* some ousfruit from one of the stalls. All of a sudden I felt a hand on my arm ... He caught me stealing. But he let me go.'

Tempika looked at his feet. 'Well, you were, what? Sixteen? It didn't seem right. The punishment for stealing is to lose a hand.'

'Mate.' Ryan grimaced.

'I know. I'd never seen a mixed person before. I thought they were a myth. Breeding between human and loba is the worst form of sin, or so I'd been told. We're taught that a child like Jaya is an abomination. But I … I just thought she was the most beautiful girl I'd ever seen.'

Jaya laughed and ruffled his hair. 'Oh you big featherheart! Obviously I'd grown up with Mother and Father and the resistance, but I'd come to expect humans – and especially monks – to be hateful bigots. So Tem came as something of a surprise. A wonderful surprise.'

'Of course then she stalked me …' Tempika gave her a nudge.

'I didn't *stalk* you! I may have *followed* you on some of your patrols … I was curious about this strange monk who'd shown me such kindness.'

'And of course, I couldn't get her out of my head. She's taught me so much. As have Pry and Mariya.'

Mariya looked on. 'I can't wait to call him my son,' she said warmly.

'What about you and Pry?' Ryan asked her.

'Many, many moons ago, we were in the same mixed orphanage in Kanda City. Childhood sweethearts.' Her eyes went misty as she vanished down memory lane. 'Funny, isn't it? As children we haven't yet learned who we're supposed to hate.'

Her words hit Yaz like a brick to the chest. She remembered how Poppy Hillman stopped being her best friend once they got to high school because Taylor Grant said she was an 'Islamist terrorist'. Still hurt, nearly ten years later, a stabbing pain under her ribs.

Mariya went on. 'When I look at Jaya and Tem I feel such hope for the future. Every once in a while I dare to imagine an end to all this.'

It was a nice idea, thought Yaz, but hatred always seems to find a way through the cracks.

The Doctor practically danced around the reading room, her coat tails spinning. 'It's absolutely, a hundred per cent, entirely, wholly true. I am the Time Lord known as the Doctor. I travel through time and space with my friends, dedicating my long life to spreading harmony and joy, and ending conflict. Oh and sunsets. You can never, ever, see enough sunsets.'

On this, the third retelling, Graham thought Mykados's red face might really pop. 'Stop this blasphemy!'

'But I'm right! It's your books that are wrong! You can either listen to my lived experience of events, or continue to rely on scraps of centuries-old paper! Which will it be?'

'To question the Word is heresy!'

'To *not* question things is stupidity!' The Doctor jabbed Mykados in the chest. 'For the last time. I did come here once before, six hundred years ago. I did *not* leave behind a list of rules, Mykados. They're invented; fictional; lies to suit the leading class and subjugate everyone else!'

'Enough!'

'It *is* enough! Six hundred years of cruelty in my name is six hundred too many. It ends now!'

'I said enough!' Mykados picked up a bronze statuette of the Good Doctor – a surprisingly good likeness – off his desk and hurled it at the Doctor. She ducked out of the way, and it left an imprint in the wood panelling behind her. Graham shot to his feet and went to the Doctor's side.

The Doctor blinked. 'Oi. Stroppy.'

'Guards!' Mykados shouted. 'Guards!' Three Temple guards burst into the room on his command. 'Seize this woman!'

The guards grabbed hold of the Doctor, pinning her arms to her sides. She rolled her eyes. 'Oh let go. I'm not doing anything.'

'Take her to the cells!'

'You're locking me up now? What for?'

Mykados, red in the face and sweating profusely, stepped out from behind his desk. 'For a human to claim to be the divine Good Doctor is a crime under the laws of the Temple. For a woman to claim to be the Good Doctor is the foulest, most disgusting parody of our religion.'

'Sorry,' said the Doctor holding up a finger. 'Can I just ask what the problem with women is? You don't seem right keen.'

His eyes narrowed. 'The moral weakness of women brought about the near extinction of Lobos.'

'Oh, that old chestnut. Or indeed, that old apple.'

'Be silent.' Mykados took a deep breath. 'You have committed a heinous crime. And the sentence is death.'

Chapter 14

The guard clamped a heavy metal collar around the Doctor's neck. There were already chains around her wrists, attached to either wall of a dank cell. For such a slight person, it was overkill, thought Graham. The dungeon was rank: water ran down the walls and mice scurried across the floor.

'Well, if you're the god you claim to be, get out of those,' Mykados said.

The Doctor glowered up at him. 'I never said I was a god. Never.'

Graham felt worse than useless, watching on, a guard's hand clamped on his shoulder.

'You have twelve hours to confess your sins before the Good Doctor. Then you will face the gravest earthly punishment, and I only hope the Good Doctor is able to forgive you and allow you to enter the kingdom of Tordos.'

Mykados then turned on Graham. 'As for you, I have questions. Guard, take him to the interrogation room.'

'Wait!' Graham wriggled out of the guard's grasp and ran to the Doctor. 'Are you OK? What can I do?'

The Doctor gave him a half-smile. 'Just tell them the truth. Maybe he'll listen. Maybe he won't, but at least we were honest.'

'What about you?' The guard grabbed him, dragging him away.

'Well I'm not going anywhere am I?' She tugged on her chains. 'Can't even reach my pocket.' That, he knew, was code for *I can't get to my sonic.*

'I'll do what I can!' he cried.

The Doctor now grinned widely. 'You might not be the Good Doctor, Graham, but you're a helluva good man!'

The door slammed shut behind him.

After being frogmarched out of the dungeon, Graham was pushed into yet another cell and tied into a freezing cold granite throne, covered in tell-tale rust-brown stains. Leather straps cut into his wrists. The only saving grace was they were now above sea level and some natural light filtered in through high bars. The whole room reeked. Graham could do nothing but try to breathe through his mouth.

'Confess,' Mykados said, prowling around Graham like a panther. 'Confess your sins.'

Graham craned his neck around. 'Look, mate, I never said I was your Good Doctor – it was your Eye things that recognised me.'

The priest leaned over him, got right in his face. He had bad breath. 'How did you do that? How did you bewitch them?'

'I didn't bewitch nothing! The Eyes recognised me because we been here before. Simple as that. There were pictures! There were!'

'Brother Lazar …?' Mykados said, and a very skinny, gaunt monk wheeled a tray of surgical instruments forward. Razor-sharp scalpels and saws glistened in the pale light.

'Crikey!' Graham's eyes nearly popped out of his head. 'There's no need to torture me! I'll tell you anything you want! I'm an open book!'

'How did you steal the likeness of the Good Doctor?'

'I didn't steal my own ruddy face!' Graham snapped.

Brother Lazar selected a long sharp needle.

'Wait!' Graham pleaded, squirming on the cold block. 'I'll tell you everything, and I'll be honest, but just tell him to put the knitting needle away!'

Mykados held up a hand and Lazar replaced the implement.

'I am sorry I played along with the Good Doctor thing. I shouldn't have done that. Fairly obviously, I am not the Good Doctor.'

'I knew it!'

He adopted a softer tone, speaking only to Mykados. 'But you're going to need an open mind, mate. What really happened is every bit as unlikely as me being a god.'

Mykados folded his arms. 'Very well. Proceed.'

Graham wriggled on the seat. He'd get piles if they kept him here long. 'OK. That blue box. The one that went missing from the grove – that's a time machine.'

A single eyebrow shot up at the corner. 'A time machine?'

'Yeah. It's a spaceship that travels in time. I know, it sounds bonkers! Believe you me, I took some convincing too! But it's true. Yesterday my friend – the woman downstairs – brought us to Lobos.'

'Yesterday?'

'Yesterday for us, six hundred years ago for you.'

'Because ... you're a time traveller?'

'Yes. I said it sounded nuts, but it don't make it any less true. When we left, there was a truce between humans and loba. I swear. We only came back because Lord Ra ... because Ryan left his phone behind. Something must've gone wrong because we shot forward in time. That's why you recognise me, mate. I've been here before.'

'But you no longer claim to be the Good Doctor?'

He shook his head. 'Mykados, there's no good way to say this, but there is no Good Doctor,' he said as gently as he could. 'It's just her downstairs. She helped the humans and loba to make some sort of peace agreement. She's amazing, but she's not a god.'

Mykados's face twisted in rage. 'I should cut out your tongue for that.'

There was a knock on the heavy cell door.

'Enter!'

The door opened and a trio of monks entered: two older ones and Ryan's little mate ... Tempika, was it? 'Your Grace.'

'Father, Brothers? What troubles you?'

One of the older monks – who looked exactly as Graham imagined a monk to look with his flowing white beard – stepped forward. 'High Priest Mykados, word has reached the Temple that you plan to execute one of the newcomers?'

'You are not mistaken. She will be executed for acts of terrible blasphemy.'

The older monks looked at each uncomfortably. Graham tried to slip his hand out of the restraint. What he'd actually do if he got free was another question. He reckoned he could probably take Mykados if it was a one-on-one deal. No good, though, the bands were so tight he could feel them cutting off the circulation to his hands. He was going nowhere.

'There is … a sense of unease,' said the third monk. 'Many of the younger brothers feel … well they still believe our guests are divine beings.'

'They are *liars* and *heathens*,' Mykados spat.

The bearded one spoke again. 'After what we all witnessed at the East Mines, they question if this is a test of our faith, Your Grace.'

Mykados threw his hands in the air. 'It is a test of my patience, Father Ornid!'

'All the same …'

'All the same *nothing*! This imbecile has even admitted he's not the Good Doctor! He's mortal! As human as you or I!'

'Oi!' Graham snapped. 'Human, yes, but I think imbecile is a bit strong!'

Father Ornid held up a crooked finger. 'But isn't that what he'd say if it was a test of our faith, Your Grace?'

'If that woman in the dungeon is truly a divine being, our Good Doctor here will surely intervene on her behalf won't he? Will he see his angel beheaded?'

'Well I'm not sure that's how faith works, Your Grace.'

Mykados struck Father Ornid with the back of his hand. 'You dare to call *my* faith into question, Father?'

Ornid looked like he might strike back for a second, but then bowed away, instead glaring at his boss.

Tempika cleared his throat. 'Your Grace? Does it not say in the Book of Truths, in Justice, that when a traveller, fool or child comes to Lobos, unfamiliar with the Book of Truths, it is our holy responsibility to educate them in the ways of the Good Doctor? These newcomers strike me as all three. They don't know our laws.'

'Your Grace,' the third monk spoke again. 'I don't know what the younger monks will do if you proceed with the execution. There's talk of a rebellion – the Brothers of Rasmin House in particular.'

'Reformists and woolly liberals,' Mykados sneered.

'And you can't kill all of us, Mykados,' Father Ornid said, clutching his cheek. 'Oh yes, don't think for a single second we don't know what really happened to Brother Carteris after he spoke out.'

'I don't know *what* you speak of.'

This was interesting, Graham thought. Maybe Mykados wasn't as in control as he thought. Dissent in the ranks and all that. He mentally filed that away for later – could come in handy.

'Very well. Let the brethren come and witness this sham for what it really is.' Mykados smiled a rodent-like smile, and Graham acutely wanted to knock his block off. 'Here's a compromise. Let us instead sentence the woman blasphemer to trial by combat, as set out in the Book of Truths. Yes, I like that. If these interlopers are immortal, she'll make short work of Tromos, won't she?'

All three monks stiffened. 'Tromos, Your Grace?' From their tone, Graham didn't like the sound of that one bit.

'Yes. Tell the guards to ready him and take him to the old arena in Kanda.'

'But the arena's been derelict for years!' Tempika argued. 'And Tromos … Tromos will pulverise her!'

'Yes, Brother Tempika. Yes he will.'

Chapter 15

Mayor Belen swept down the marble hallway, tying his robe as he went. The kerfuffle had woken Ana, and he would no doubt feel her wrath when morning came. Mykados waited from him on the terrace. Three white moons rippled on a black sea. In his mind's eye, Belen envisaged pushing the priest over the railings and down the cliffs.

He immediately prayed the Good Doctor for forgiveness in his head.

'Mykados,' he said, barely concealing his annoyance. 'What is the meaning of this? It's the middle of the night. I told you I'd make a public address about the events that unfolded at the East Mines *in the morning*.'

The vulture-like head bowed slightly. 'I am truly sorry, Mayor Belen. I'm afraid there have been further developments that simply couldn't wait until dawn.'

'Go ahead,' Belen sighed, before shouting over his shoulder: 'Rex! Fetch me caffa!' Inside the villa, he heard Rex shuffle towards the kitchens.

'I've come to seek your permission to reopen the fighting arena at Kanda.'

'What? Why on earth would you do that?' The rebels had used some chemical weapon on the site about ten years ago, before he'd become Mayor. The last he heard, the ground was dangerously radioactive.

'One of the newcomers, a woman of all things, is claiming to be the true Good Doctor. The penalty for such blasphemy is death, but in the ... unusual circumstances ... it's felt that to execute her outright may not be appropriate.'

'A woman?'

'Indeed.'

'And how do you know she's lying? You said yourself that the Good Doctor's return was foretold. Perhaps the outward appearance—'

'He would return *as a man!*' Mykados's eyes were close to popping out of his skull. 'You have seen the artworks and artefacts from the dark days. You have seen the Image! When the Good Doctor came to Lobos it was as a *man.*'

'But he's a ... mystical being. Could he not change his face?'

'Mayor Belen! To even suggest such a thing!' Mykados's face twisted into a pained scowl. 'In the scriptures of High Priest Klaxa, he clearly sets out how the weakness of women, their wanton nature, led to the Great Plague. The impure breeding of human and loba almost destroyed our way of life forever. Women are simply *inferior*. How could the Good Doctor ever be something so lowly when he is the best of everything we understand?'

That sort of thinking had never sat especially well with Belen. He loved women. Sometimes too much, he thought. But he'd also learned there was no arguing with Mykados. 'The fighting arena has been shut for years, I thought …'

'That it was still radioactive? Not so according to our survey from last year. It's quite safe.'

Belen rubbed his eyes. 'Isn't it a little … archaic, Mykados?' He keenly remembered some of the trials of combat from back in the day, and they were a gruesome spectacle.

'Not at all!' Mykados said. 'And the fights were a source of income. What did we used to charge for a ticket? Fifteen Golds? More? Oh and the old families loved it so. All of the founders and merchants would bring their children. I think, during these troubled times, it could be a very *popular* move on the part of the Mayor.'

That woke him up. 'Well I suppose it could be good for community morale.'

'Precisely.'

'Just make it, quick, yes? We don't need too much … gore and suchlike. Think of the children.'

'I think it'll be good for the people of Old Town and beyond to see what becomes of those who would impersonate our saviour.' He held up his hands. 'But fear not. I have selected Tromos as the Temple's champion. The blasphemer won't last long.'

'Tromos!' Belen cried. 'Are you out of your mind?'

'I beg your pardon?'

'I … I'm sorry … I just mean. Tromos is a savage … a *monster*. Is letting him out of his cage a good idea?'

'Oh yes.' A hint of a smile curled Mykados's lips. 'There isn't a child in Old Town who isn't aware of Tromos. They tell stories around the fire about the soldier who became a living nightmare. So … let's give them something to talk about.'

'Heeeeeeeelp meeeeeeee!'

The woman in the dungeon had been wailing at the Eye guarding her for about ten minutes now, and Gadapolos was monitoring them by himself. He reluctantly trudged down the dank stairs into the dungeon. It *stank* down here – of what, he dreaded to think.

He reached the cell and peered through the observation hatch. She was a slight, impish woman, but appearances can be deceptive. They'd taught him that on his first day of guard training. Plus which – although he hadn't been there – he had heard rumours about what happened at the East Mines. This woman could be a god, or a witch, or both.

'Pleeeeeeease!' she cried again.

With a sigh, Gadapolos unlocked and unbolted the door. 'What do you want?' He could do without this. With all the excitement up at the mines, his replacement hadn't come to relieve him so it looked like he was stuck working a double shift. He hadn't even had a tea break. His seachicken sandwich was untouched in his locker.

'Oh, thank goodness.' The strange woman wrinkled her face up. 'I've got a really bad itch on my nose and I can't reach it!' She nodded at the hovering Eye. 'And I don't want that thing anywhere near my face. Please! This is torture, and I'd know, frankly!'

'You have an itchy nose?'

'A *really* itchy nose. Will you come give it a little scratch?'

Gadapolos bristled. 'No! Who knows what you'll do!'

The woman frowned at him. 'You're kidding, aren't you? I'm strung up like a puppet! What could I possibly do? Oh come on, it costs nothing to do a kindness.'

'Oh, for crying out loud.' She was right. He was younger than her, but towered over her and, unless she was a witch, there was no way she was getting out of those chains. But what if she *was* a witch? 'I warn you, I'm armed and ready to use maximum force.' He readied his stun gun.

'Oh, put that down, you're not scratching my nose with that thing.'

He inched forward towards her.

'It's not getting any less itchy …'

Gadapolos reached forward with his index finger and scratched the tip of her nose.

'Ooh, bit lower!' He did so. 'Aaaah, that's the spot. I'm not, but if I was the Good Doctor, you'd be straight into the fictional land of Tordos. Good lad.'

He rolled his eyes. She seemed harmless. 'You shouldn't say that. It's why you're here.'

'But I'm not the Good Doctor,' she said with a grin. 'I'm just the Doctor. Maybe I'm *a* good Doctor, but not *the* Good Doctor. There are lots and lots of us all the world over, doing all sorts of good doctoring.'

'The Good Doctor has watched over Lobos for centuries,' he said matter-of-factly.

She narrowed her shrewd eyes. He wondered if she was cleverer than she looked. 'Do you believe that, though? That there's a magical man keeping you all safe?'

He thought about it for a moment. He looked over his shoulder; he could get in deep trouble for saying what he was about to say. 'I don't know. But the stories are nice. I grew up with them. My mother used to tell us the stories at bedtime.'

The woman smiled. 'Oh, I'm full of stories. Would you like to hear one?'

Gadapolos shrugged. It was the start of his second shift and he had a long night ahead. 'Why not?'

The woman smiled. 'Good lad! Once upon a time, there were four best friends and they travelled very, very far from home. They saw all sorts of amazing and wonderful things until one day they came to a world at war. Two types of people were arguing over who owned the rocks, the sand, the sea.'

'No one owns those things.'

'Well quite. Each side thought they were superior to the other. Not just in weaponry and strength, but in their blood and bones.' She looked into his eyes, not letting him go. Gadapolos was transfixed. 'And that's the funny thing, because after all the death, when the bodies were piled high, both sides looked on in horror and saw the truth ...'

Gadapolos shifted uncomfortably. 'And what was that?'

'That bone is white and blood is red.'

Pry gathered everyone in the main cavern for a progress report. He stood on a boulder, looming over the rest of the resistance. 'Brothers and sisters! I have the latest geological reports. Dayna hacked into the comms network and it's even better than we hoped. The blast in the East Mine has dramatically destabilised the whole structure of the mines.'

Ryan was confused again. They had the Eyes and the nifty buggy things here, but in other ways the society seemed pretty primitive. 'What network?' he asked Jaya, who was between him and Yaz, listening to the address.

'A few years ago, the Mayor and the Temple agreed to limit radio and telecommunications to hinder us,' she explained. 'But they still do a daily transmission from the Temple to all the other towns and ports on Lobos. We have enough salvaged equipment from before the ban to listen in.'

'Are we safe down here?' one of the human fighters shouted up at Pry.

'Yes. We think so. Although we'll stay close to the surface and to the west of Old Town.'

'So what now?' Jaya called up at her father.

'We proceed into the heart of the caves underneath the Temple.'

'But hold up!' Ryan shouted up. 'Won't we all be buried alive? Not loving that plan, to be honest.'

Pry shook his head. 'Valid concern. One crew will take the excavator forward, while a second stabilises the new tunnels to create an escape route. I don't want to lose another life. We already lost Daley at the prison and it's not good enough. We've all worked for so long towards this day, and now I can see it. You and me … we're going to destroy the totem of six hundred years of oppression!'

There was an almighty cheer from the crowd.

Ryan put up his hand, like he was still at school. 'Excuse me?'

'Ryan?' Pry looked down, unimpressed.

'Sorry, but … erm … what then?'

'What do you mean?'

'So you pull down the Temple, and then what? They won't just give up power.'

'No one ever does,' Yaz added.

'While the Temple is in chaos, we make our move. We'll remove that spineless weasel Belen from power and seize control of Old Town. Our brothers and sisters in the provinces will do the same.'

Another huge cheer, people chanted Pry's name over and over. Ryan gently pulled Yaz out of the crowd.

'What?' she said.

'They're just the same,' he told her.

She frowned. 'Who are?'

'The Temple and this lot. He just said it – more brothers and sisters!'

'I'll grant you I've not actually been in the Temple yet, but come on,' she said. 'The Temple has been telling everyone for hundreds of years that *we* told them women and loba were an underclass or something. You can't blame them for being a little cheesed off.'

'I *have* seen 'em both, and they sound exactly the same. Like cults. One of them worships the Good Doctor, this lot worships Pry.'

Yaz sighed. 'Or the cause.'

'A cause that's gonna *cause* a massive earthquake! How do they know they aren't gonna get anyone hurt? Are they, like, a bit stupid, or do they just not care?'

'I know. I know. I want to help the loba, I do, but I also know this isn't the right way to go about it. It'll be a disaster.'

Ryan looked over his shoulder at the rebels, all still clapping and cheering at whatever Pry was saying. 'So what do we do?'

'We do what the Doctor did last time. Somehow we've got to get everyone around a table to talk. It worked back then, didn't it?'

Ryan didn't even see Tempika slipping into the cavern until he was right under his nose. 'Ryan, Yasmin, I came as soon as I could.' His face was clammy and pale. He was out of breath like he'd sprinted here.

'Why? What's up?' Ryan said.

'Take a minute, you're OK,' said Yaz.

'We don't have a minute,' Tempika panted. 'I've come from the jail. I did everything I could, I swear.'

'Tempika, what's going on?' Ryan's stomach sank.

'They've sentenced the Doctor to trial by combat. Against Tromos …'

'Tromos!' Yaz exclaimed.

That name again. 'What's Tromos?' Ryan said.

'You don't wanna know,' Yaz said. 'Ryan … he's going to kill her.'

Chapter 16

The Doctor looked ridiculously small compared to the five hulking guards who transported her, with a sack over her head, to the fighting arena. She had no idea how far they'd come in the buggy, but she sensed they were probably on the outskirts of Old Town.

Now on foot, she was frogmarched into tunnels underneath the stadium that smelled only faintly nicer than the dungeon. With a firm shove, she staggered forward and the sack was pulled off her head. 'Hello!' she said.

It was daylight and she was in another cell, this one filled with rusty weapons. Everything was covered with orange dust and cobwebs. The air felt stale, like it hadn't been breathed in a long time.

'Fighter,' said a guard. 'Choose your weapon.'

'I beg your pardon?'

'As it is said in the Book of Truths, you will face the Good Doctor's current champion in the holy arena. The High Priest has decreed that the prisoner Tromos will now take on that mantle.'

'Oh, I just bet he has.'

The guard ignored her. 'If the Good Doctor's fortune smiles down upon you, you may live on to see another sunrise. Your fate is in his hands.'

'If that's true, then we're all doomed,' she said with a smile.

'Fighter. Choose your weapon. Spear, sword or dagger?'

Hands secured behind her back, she scanned the rows of deadly looking blades. 'Is "shield" not an option?'

'No.'

'In that case, I'm all right, thanks for asking.'

'Choose a weapon.'

'No thank you.'

The guard looked at her with a mixture of pity and revulsion. 'Simpleton! To face Tromos is a death sentence, to face him unarmed is madness.'

The Doctor shrugged. 'Well if it's a death sentence, a pointy bit of metal isn't going to make much of a difference is it?'

'Imbecile.' The guard turned to his colleague. 'Put her in the holding cell next to the arena.'

'One thing,' said the Doctor. 'Can this prison at least have a window?'

Mykados entered Graham's cell flanked by a pair of Temple guards.

'Oi! What's going on?' Graham said. 'No one's telling me anything!' And his bum was now totally numb.

'The trial by combat will commence shortly. I came to ask if you'd like to witness the demise of your friend.'

Graham scowled. 'You never had a single girlfriend at school, did you?'

He swore he saw Mykados flinch. He ignored his question. 'Well? What is it to be?'

'Oh I want to see this,' Graham tried to sound as brave as possible. 'She always thinks of something. She'll get out of it, she always does.' More to the point, they'd have to untie him to get him to this trial. Once he was free, he could try to come up with a plan of attack.

'Such faith,' Mykados said with a sneer. 'But misplaced. Release him,' he told the guards.

The guard undid the strap on his left wrist and was making a start on the right, when the room started to shake. This was no mere tremor. The quake felt close, like something enormous was moving just under their feet. Dust started to rain down onto his head. 'Quick!' Graham said. 'Get me out before this whole place ...'

A huge chunk of masonry came loose and crashed down. Mykados threw himself out of the way, narrowly avoiding being crushed.

Graham winced and waited for the ceiling to come smashing down on them. The quake subsided. He took a deep breath. Next to him, the guard seemed equally shaken.

Covered in thick dust, Mykados rose to his feet, brushing off his robes.

The other guard helped him up. 'Your Grace? Do you require the medic?'

'No, no, I'm all right.'

'Your Grace ... these earthquakes ... they're getting worse.'

'Yes, yes I can see that! I'm sorry, my child, I don't mean to scold. It seems the Good Doctor, the real Doctor in Tordos, is gravely displeased with us. This is His punishment. For our worship of this false god ...'

Graham was forced upright by the guard. 'Oh, what a load of utter—'

'It is said in the Book of Truths that the Good Doctor would return at the end of time. The last days of Lobos, when the tug of the twin suns splits the earth in two.' Mykados circled Graham. His voice dripped with spite. 'I don't know who or what you are, but this cannot be a coincidence. The Good Doctor is furious we fell so quickly for your lies. One can only pray that the death of the woman who calls herself the Doctor eases the wrath below our feet.'

'Killing us won't change earthquakes, you flamin' moron!'

As if the earth could hear him, there was another tremor, an aftershock perhaps.

'If the Good Doctor demands it, then we shall all finally leave this physical realm, with all its death and pain, and join him in Tordos. We cannot question His word. Now come. The fighting arena awaits.'

'It's an earthquake, mate! You should be concentrating on saving the town ... move them to the other side of Lobos or something!'

'I just told you, it is not our place to challenge His divine will. If it is the foretold time, we must all accept our fate.'

And that was when Graham truly saw it. This little old man wasn't some kind old grandpa teaching a bit of

Sunday School. He was a flipping lunatic. And that meant they were all in very deep trouble.

Yaz had been arguing with Pry for some time now and he didn't seem to be listening. 'Pry, please! We have to stop the fight! Tromos will kill her! He nearly choked me to death with one hand and a door between us!'

He ignored her. 'No. We're so close now. We can't afford the time.'

'Of course you can! This has been going on for six hundred years, what's a few more hours?'

Mariya stepped in. 'Oh, Pry, come on. She's right. If this Doctor woman is an enemy of the Temple, she's a friend of ours.'

'I said no! I'm not risking my people to save the neck of a stranger.'

'She's not a stranger,' Ryan added. 'She saved Lobos from civil war once. And she can do it again.'

'She can help you!' Yaz took hold of Pry's big paws, but he pulled them back. She pointed at where the TARDIS still rested on the trolley. 'Listen. If I could fly that thing, I *would* take you back. Not to kill anyone but to see when there was peace. When we left here, there was a truce between loba and humans and that's because of the Doctor. Because of all of us.'

Pry shook his head. 'Yasmin, you have a good heart, but I think we've gone past diplomacy. During the Great Plague, did you know loba were rounded up and shot to curb the spread of disease? Great pyres of our bodies burned while humans stood around and cheered.'

'Hashtag not all humans!' Ryan said. 'You're married to one!'

'Exactly! Isn't that what you want?' said Yaz. 'For everyone to live together? This isn't as simple as us and them!'

'Especially when I'm both,' Jaya said very quietly.

Pry looked to his feet and Yaz wondered if, under his fur, he was blushing in shame.

'And the Temple's use of Tromos is slavery,' Mariya said. 'It's disgusting. When I think about the suffering he's been through, my blood boils. We could free him and this Doctor at the same time.'

Jaya pointed down one of the many tunnels that led off the main camp. 'Come on, Father. We're only about a kilometre from the old fighting arena. If we can get back into the sewer system, all we have to do is disrupt the trial – set off a smoke bomb or something and then retrieve her. It'll be easy.'

'Please,' Yaz said again.

Pry growled. 'Fine. But just a small team. Us and a couple more fighters. And I'm not risking this turning into a gunfight like at the prison. Look what happened to poor Daley. We'll create the diversion, then it's up to you.' He glowered down at Yaz. 'If she's so important, you can put your lives on the line.'

Chapter 17

The afternoon suns were high in the sky and it was baking hot away from the cool breeze on the coast. A buggy drove Graham, Mykados and the guards across a sandy, arid landscape. Graham saw vast pink-coloured lizards basking on rocks in the sunshine.

This district looked like it has been abandoned. There were burnt-out vehicles at the side of the road, and some old houses and a shopping centre were derelict. The arena didn't look much better. Once it must have been quite grand, but now tattered flags hung limp and the huge billboards were torn. Graham wondered what sort of sports they used to play here in better times. A shell of a fast food restaurant still stood just outside the stadium, bright red plastic chairs half buried in the sand.

This used to be like home. Looked like it was fun once. Now it seemed the only thing still standing was that big blue Temple.

War, he thought. What is it good for?

'It's good to be back, isn't it?' Mykados told the guard. 'When did we last have a trial by combat?'

'Oh, not since the rebels used their dirty bomb.'

Well, that explained why the area had been abandoned, Graham thought. As they drove past trailers and mobile homes, clothes and bedsheets still billowed on washing lines, thick with orange dust. Everyone must have run for the hills, leaving everything behind.

As the buggy pulled into the entrance, dozens of birds took flight from the rafters. Shards of light shone through big holes in the foyer ceiling. The floor was caked in bird droppings, and Graham thought it was a very long time, years, since the arena had been used.

'I think the town elders are especially looking forward to this,' Mykados said chirpily to his escort. 'They've been campaigning for years to get the arena up and running. Ensure it's cleaned up. Use as many men as it takes. They can't see it like this, let's get it ready for the show.'

'The *show*?' Graham said with disgust. 'You're talking about watching a woman get ripped to pieces. What's wrong with you?' The guard pulled him down off the buggy by his handcuffs.

A second, larger, vehicle emerged from a cloud of sand. This one seemed to be a prison transporter with bars over the windows. Graham wondered if it was the Doctor arriving but, as it pulled through the arched entrance, he saw the whole truck was shaking.

'What's that?' he said.

From within, there came a deep, guttural roar. The van rocked from side to side like something was throwing itself against the walls. Something large.

'Oh, it's awake,' Mykados said dismissively.

'Do you want us to sedate him, Your Grace?' the guard asked.

'Absolutely not. The last thing anyone wants to see is a drowsy warrior. Is he fitted with a control collar?'

'Yes, Your Grace, naturally.'

'Then use it to keep him in line. Chain him in a holding cell until the audience is here.'

'Very well.'

The creature within the truck howled once more. 'Let me out of here! I can't breathe! Let me out!' A fist punched the side, leaving a massive dent in the metal.

'That's who the Doctor's fighting?' Graham said, his heart wedged in his throat.

'Oh yes,' Mykados said. 'That's Tromos, all right.'

Graham felt sick. He really, *really* hoped the Doctor had something up her sleeve.

The guard held the sonic screwdriver up to the light. 'And what is this?'

'Oh that old thing,' replied the Doctor. 'That's nothing. Just a screwdriver.' The Doctor was now wearing cumbersome brown leather armour over her T-shirt.

One guard looked to the other. 'Could it be used as a weapon?'

The other guarded shrugged. 'I'm not sure, but it's certainly not a spear, sword or dagger. Therefore it's forbidden in combat.'

The guard rested the sonic on top of the Doctor's coat where it lay on a bench. The Doctor sighed. That was about a third of her plans scuppered.

*

Two sewers in twenty-four hours, thought Yaz, how lucky am I? At least this one had standing room and they were able to run – or in her case limp – at full height underneath the Kanda arena.

'The arena hasn't been used for about six years,' Jaya explained, jogging alongside her. 'We used to come here when I was little for the annual Physicalia Tournament.'

'Only then the new Mayor came in to power and they said loba weren't allowed in the arena any more,' Mariya said. 'Things were bad and then they got worse.'

Yaz nodded. Progress never was made in a straight line. She guessed, as on Earth, there were peaks and troughs on the path to equality.

Up ahead, Pry held up an arm. 'Quiet!' he hissed.

Yaz reached his position. It was just them, Pry and his family, and Dayna, a loba with bright ginger fur and emerald green eyes. Ryan was some way further down the tunnel, taking extra care not to go face down in raw sewage. Yaz looked up through a metal grille and saw feet passing by overhead, and voices, a din of voices. 'Who are they?'

'We're directly below the arena,' Pry explained. 'So keep your voices down.'

Ryan finally caught them up with Tempika. 'What's going on?'

'We're here,' Yaz said.

'Is this when we set off the smoke bomb thing?'

'No,' Pry hissed. 'We have to wait until the fight has begun. She'll be under close guard until then. Look, there's already dozens of guards up there.'

Jaya and Dayna fixed some sort of grenade-type-thing to a ladder with tape. Yaz guessed it was a remote-controlled smoke bomb. 'No one will get hurt, right?'

'The gas stings the eyes a little,' Jaya said. 'Nothing serious.'

Yaz looked at Ryan and nodded. The more smoke the better. Hopefully it'd make it harder for guards to shoot at them.

'Keep going,' Mariya said. 'There should be a storm drain in the tunnel that leads into the arena itself. That's the closest we can get. You might have to blast your way into the fighting pit.'

Pry led the way. 'It's all about timing. When the canisters go off, you'll have seconds to get in the arena and get your friend down the drain. As soon as the guards work out what's happening, they'll kill the lot of you.'

'We'll have you covered,' Mariya said.

'You're not going in,' Pry growled. 'Their friend, their problem.'

'Oh don't be ridiculous, Pry. They're unarmed and untrained.'

'And what about Tromos?' Yaz said. 'He'll be on the loose.'

Pry smiled. 'That's why I brought Dayna.'

'I'm a hacker,' she explained. 'I should be able to override his control collar – at least for a few minutes.'

'And he's bound to be wearing one,' said Mariya. 'There's no other way they'd have got him here. Poor old Tromos.'

'With him we assess the situation,' Pry said. 'If – if – there's a way we can extract him safely, we will. I can't babysit a botched Temple experiment when we're so close …'

Yaz felt butterflies gurgle in her stomach. This was madness, but she remembered Tromos's hand around her throat. There was no way she could leave the Doctor to face him alone. She looked ahead at Pry, and prayed she could trust him to get them out of the arena alive.

The doors opened as dusk set in, and the arena filled quickly. The amphitheatre rows were chockfull, about half were monks from the Temple, and the other half looked to be very wealthy-looking townsfolk. Some had even brought their children to spectate. They waited impatiently, fidgeting, little gold binoculars at the ready.

Graham was with Mykados in some sort of VIP box right at eye-level to the fight. They had the best seats in the house. He was still handcuffed.

An excited hum of anticipation grew. 'TROMOS! TROMOS! TROMOS!' the crowd chanted. The poor Doctor was up against the home team by the sounds of it.

A guard approached. 'Your Grace. The arena is at capacity, two thousand people, and the combatants are in place. We're ready to begin.'

'Excellent.' Mykados looked to Graham. He smiled snidely. 'And now all of Lobos will see what becomes of traitors of the Temple.'

Graham ground his back teeth together. He was gonna nut this bloke first chance he got.

Mykados stepped down from their box and strode into the middle of the arena. A microphone was ready for him on a little podium. A respectful hush fell over the crowd and the chanting ceased.

'Praise be.'

'Praise the Good Doctor!' the crowd recited robotically.

Mykados held up a hand. 'My friends. Welcome back to the Arena of Justice. It is said in the Book of Truths, Justice 9, that it is an unforgiveable sin to deny the Word of the Good Doctor, and an even more grave crime to claim to be on a par with His greatness. The slovenly woman you are about to witness committed the most heinous blasphemy. She claimed to *be* the Good Doctor!'

The audience gasped, covering their mouths with their hands.

Mykados shook his head. 'The Good Doctor, a woman? Can you even imagine such a travesty?'

Some roared with laughter, some yelled 'No!' Someone definitely cried out 'Kill her!' Graham looked at the crowd with sheer disgust. Bloodthirsty animals.

'And now the time has come for her judgment. As it was in the glory days, the lying infidel will be given one chance to earn her redemption in combat. The Temple's champion, Tromos, will defend the word of the Good Doctor. And only fate can save the heathen now. If the Good Doctor wishes it so, she will be protected under His forgiving and benevolent gaze.'

The crowd cheered and Graham swore he could see the bloodlust in their eyes. It was like Saturday at Upton Park, except they weren't here to see West Ham, they were here to see a woman get torn limb from limb. Why weren't they stopping this? Couldn't they see how wrong it was?

'Please take your seats and enjoy fair and just trial by combat! Pray for the Good Doctor's mercy!' Mykados returned to his seat.

'Mykados, mate,' Graham said. 'It's not too late. You can stop this.'

'Only the Good Doctor can save her now.' Mykados smiled at him, voice oozing sarcasm. 'If you're my god, you'll stop it.'

'I'm telling you the truth. *She* is the Good Doctor. Well, *a* good person called the Doctor. She really is! And she can help you, bring peace back to Lobos. She's done it once before.'

Mykados dismissed him with a waft of his hand. 'The rebels are dead, buried beneath the East Mines. Once this woman is dead and you're in the prison, peace will be restored.'

The earth trembled. Out here in the desert, it wasn't so bad, but it was a little reminder. Graham saw Mykados grip his seat. His smug expression fell.

A shriek of feedback wailed around the amphitheatre. An announcer spoke. 'People of Lobos: we present the defendant. An off-worlder known only as the Nurse.'

The crowd started to boo and hiss as a metal gate slid open, and Graham saw guards shove the Doctor into the arena. She squinted against the sun like she hadn't been outside in a while. She wore a heavy tan leather vest but she was empty-handed. Was she mad? Without a sword or shield or something, she was brown bread.

She shielded her eyes and looked to him. On seeing him, she grinned and gave a jaunty wave. Graham stood, but a guard pushed him back into his seat by the shoulder.

'And please welcome to the arena, the champion of the Temple ... the one, the mighty, the fearsome ... Tromos!'

The gate at the opposite end of the arena scraped open. Silence fell over the crowd. The tunnel was dark and empty. Graham leaned forward to get a better view.

'What's it doing?' Mykados muttered.

And then Tromos emerged.

Chapter 18

Tromos was twice the size of any other loba Graham had seen, and he was hunching. He was *huge*, his shoulders filling the entire tunnel. He stepped into the sunlight, also seemingly blinded, and Graham got a better look. His fur was black and grey, dirty and matted looking. A heavy brow sat over almost red eyes. Spittle ran from his yellow fangs onto his rough prison jumpsuit.

There was a metal collar around his neck, this one more heavy-duty than the ones the other loba wore. A tiny red light flashed intermittently. Graham looked down and saw the guard next to Mykados – Makris – held some sort of remote control. If he could reach over and get his hands on that ...

'FIGHT!' the announcer shouted, and a klaxon sounded.

Tromos growled and flexed his claws. Spraying drool, he sprinted across the sandy floor towards the Doctor, who stood completely still.

Graham wiped his palms on his trouser legs. She had to move. She *had* to move or he was going to mow her down. 'Doctor!' he shouted, although it was lost in cheers.

Maybe it was his imagination, but as Tromos grew closer to the Doctor, he seemed to slow a little, a frown creasing his brow.

He roared and raised a paw. His teeth were fully bared.

The Doctor just stood there.

Tromos threw back his head and howled. He tore off the top half of his jumpsuit to reveal rippling furry muscles. The Doctor simply stood her ground.

'You are a girl!' Tromos spat.

'Yep. These days, anyway.' Every word rang out around the auditorium. Graham realised there were microphones attached to the floodlights to amplify the screams and grunts.

'Why don't you fight?' Tromos took a swipe at her. The Doctor casually ducked back, reflexes lightning fast.

'Well!' the Doctor said, holding up a finger. 'Before we fight, I just had a few pertinent questions. I thought you might be able to clarify them, mister …?'

'I am Tromos.'

'Mister Tromos. Nice to meet you, I'm the Doctor. First of all I wondered if you could just go over the rules for me. No one bothered to actually explain them! Typical isn't it?'

Graham looked up and saw some people in the audience looking very confused.

'KILL HER!' one snooty-looking man shouted through cupped hands.

'WHAT ARE YOU WAITING FOR?' a different woman screamed.

'Fear me …' Tromos took what looked like a fairly gentle swing at her with the back of his hand but it was enough to send the Doctor flying across the arena.

In the middle of a dust cloud, the Doctor sat upright and shook the sand out of her hair. 'Oof,' she said. She got to her feet and strolled back to Tromos. 'OK. So that's the first rule? I fear you because you're big and scary? Is that right?'

'Fight, girl.'

'In a minute, hold your horses. What's the rush? These people have all paid for tickets, I'm assuming. Might as well give them their money's worth. So. In terms of fighting. What are the rules? Like what's legal? Or is it a free for all? I was once at Ultimate Fighting Champion, or was it Peladon?' She scratched her head. 'I forget. Anyway, no rules at all! Biting, spitting, nipping! Just not cricket, is it?'

Tromos looked back to Mykados, as confused as the audience.

Mykados's nostrils flared. He turned to Makris. 'Stimulate him.'

Makris turned a knob on the remote control and Tromos clutched the collar around his neck. He howled in pain. Staggering forwards, he flailed his arms around and the Doctor ducked and rolled out of the way with the greatest of ease.

'That's not cricket, either, is it? So, Mister Tromos, is that legal? They're allowed to electrocute you to provoke a more violent fight?'

Tromos fell to one knee. 'Fear me.'

The Doctor dared to take a step *closer*. 'I don't want to fight you, Mister Tromos. We're not puppets, you or I.'

Tromos snarled and charged forwards again. 'Quiet! Fool girl!'

The Doctor held out a hand. 'STOP!'

Tromos actually stopped.

'Just wait a second. Am I right in thinking this is a fight to the *death*?'

Tromos pulled at his collar, hitting at his chest. 'I. Must. Kill. You!' He kicked at the sand in frustration.

'But what happens when I'm dead, Mister Tromos?' the Doctor said calmly. 'What happens to *you*? Do you go free?' She stepped ever closer, right under his nose. 'When were you last free? Have you ever been free?'

Graham realised he was going lightheaded from forgetting to breathe.

'KILL HER! KILL HER! KILL HER! KILL HER!' The people in the crowd were now chanting and stamping their feet. Tromos was not the monster in this arena.

'Hurt him,' Mykados hissed to Captain Makris. 'I grow weary, finish this farce.'

Tromos dropped to his knees, tugging at the collar.

'I'm sorry they've done this to you, Mister Tromos, and I won't fight you. If you must, kill me, but it won't end the pain and you won't be free.'

Tromos looked up at her. 'It hurts.' It was hardly a whisper.

With a steady hand, the Doctor reached for Tromos and scratched behind his ears. 'Oh Mister Tromos,' she said and the audience audibly gasped. 'What you need is a … well, a vet, actually.'

And then the little red light on Tromos's collar went from red to green with a little bleep.

'What?' the Doctor said, her forehead creasing. 'That wasn't me …'

Tromos blinked. He rose to his feet.

'Mister Tromos?'

'Pain gone.'

'Oh…OK…well that's good,' the Doctor said cautiously.

Tromos growled, his lips curling into a smile. But instead of crushing the Doctor, he very slowly turned to face the box in which Graham was seated. Uh-oh.

'Priest.' Tromos started to jog in their direction before breaking into a full charge.

'Tromos, stop!' the Doctor cried, running after him. 'I can help you!'

'You did this.' Tromos banged his huge, swollen body with equally massive fists. 'Priest …'

'Stun him! Knock him out!' Mykados stood, backing away.

'The collar's not working!' Makris punched the controls with his fist, but they were dead.

'Guards! Open fire! Shoot to kill!' ordered Mykados.

Too late. With a mighty leap, Tromos propelled himself off the arena floor and into the audience. All around Graham, time seemed to slow down as this mutant creature flew at them.

Already people were screaming and falling over themselves to get to the exits. Bodies blocked the tunnels. It was a stampede. There was no way out.

With his deadly claws, Tromos hauled himself into the VIP box. Mykados grabbed Graham, using him as a human shield.

'Oi!' Graham yelped. 'Don't you bloody dare!' He struggled and the pair collapsed in a heap to the floor of the box.

'You turned Tromos into a beast ...' The hulk loomed over them, tearing up a row of chairs and hurling it into the arena. Spit dripped down onto Graham's face. All he could do was cover himself with his cuffed arms. 'And now I will be free ...'

Chapter 19

Graham screwed his eyes shut and waited for Tromos to toss him like a ragdoll into the crowd like he'd done the bench.

Instead there was a thundering boom and the whole stadium shook. What *now*?

Graham's ears were ringing and the auditorium was filled with screams. Opening his eyes, he saw thick grey smoke swirl and spiral into the air above him. He gasped. It was choking. His eyes started to water at once.

He heard gunfire and, a split second later, Tromos roared and blood splashed across Graham's face. Makris – Makris had opened fire on the poor sod. Tromos clutched his left shoulder with his right paw and jumped back down into the fighting pit, retreating.

Mykados pushed Graham aside and clambered to his feet. 'Guards! What's happening?'

A confused-looking young guard pushed through the crowd as they still swarmed for the exits in panic. 'Rebels! Rebel assault.'

Rebels? But they were all buried alive. Graham jumped to his feet to get a better view. He tried to see through the thick, acrid smoke that seemed to churn up through the sewers below, but it was impenetrable. Ryan. It *had* to be Ryan. And Yaz? Suddenly, Graham felt something glow in his tummy. It felt a lot like hope.

The gasmasks blocked the smell of the smoke but made it no easier to see through, and it already filled the entire arena. It was billowing up from every grate. Ryan followed Yaz, Pry and Mariya into the stadium as soon as the gate was blasted open. Jaya and Tempika were in charge of detonating the smoke bombs, Dayna was jamming the signal to Tromos's collar.

'Doctor?' Yaz called through the smog. 'Ryan, I can't see anything!'

Ryan was scared, but he certainly wasn't gonna let Yaz know that. 'Stick together. Doctor? Doctor it's us!' Gunfire. Even through the smoke, Ryan felt bullets whizz past him. *That's not good.*

'Run!' Yaz shouted. She grabbed his hand and tugged him along.

Come on, feet, Ryan thought. Let's get this right.

In the fog, they sprinted past Mariya who covered them with a gun of her own, firing blindly into the crowd. He could only hope that Graham had the sense to take cover.

'Doctor!' Ryan yelled.

'Ooh what are you shouting for?' the Doctor appeared through the mist directly beside him. 'I'm right here.'

'Doctor!' He threw his arms around her. 'Yaz! I got her!'

'Let's go!' Yaz called back.

The Doctor smiled. 'Impeccable timing! I knew you'd figure something out.' She nodded at Pry and Mariya. 'Not being funny, but did you tell them what we always say about guns?'

'They didn't listen.'

She shrugged. 'You can but try. Come on, let's get Graham and get out of—'

Another bullet whizzed past Ryan's ear. 'Quick, yeah!' He started to run back to the gate they'd come in through.

To his left there was a cry. For a second he thought it was Yaz until he saw her up ahead. She was almost at the tunnel. He turned back and saw Mariya tumble down. No! He let go of the Doctor's hand and went back to help her. 'Mariya!'

She pulled her gasmask off. 'I'm hit ... I'm hit ... my side.' She clutched the side of her torso. Blood was already spreading across her waist. It looked bad.

'Oh man! Doctor! Help her!'

He didn't know what hit him. One second he was holding Mariya up and the next his feet were off the floor. It was like he'd been flattened by a ten-tonne truck. In the smog, he could hardly tell which way up he was. Something strong crushed his chest.

'What the ...?'

The Doctor stepped in front of him. 'Tromos ... put him down.'

Ryan suddenly smelled something that strongly reminded him of wet dog. There was a strong, muscular, hairy arm hooked under his armpits. 'Doctor!'

'Stay calm, Ryan!' The Doctor held a hand out. 'Tromos, listen to me. He's a friend of mine. He means you no harm. Please ... put him down.'

More gunfire. Tromos turned and ran, still holding him. One thing he'd never, ever wanted to be was a human shield. 'Dooooooctor!' he cried, bouncing up and down as Tromos careered across the arena. Ryan was pretty tall, but Tromos carried him like he was as light as a baby. All he could do was kick his legs helplessly.

And, more to the point, what was Tromos gonna do to him when he put him down?

Trying desperately to remember that day of her training, Yaz applied pressure to the wound on Mariya's side. However hard she pressed, a pool of warm blood gushed through her fingers. Pry fired at the guards, trying to hold them off. There were kids in the crowd. Was he firing on them?

Tears stung her eyes, and it was nothing to do with the gas filling the stadium. This was chaos. Utter chaos.

The Doctor appeared at her side. 'Doctor. I can't stop it ...'

'Quickly. We have to get her out of here. Help me.' The Doctor stooped down and hooked Mariya's arm around her shoulder. Yaz did the same on the other side and together they lifted her to her feet. Mariya gasped in pain.

Yaz saw the smoke was clearing. Soon they'd be sitting ducks for the guards to take out one-by-one. 'Pry!' she screamed. 'Come on!'

As fast as they could, they half-carried, half-dragged Mariya towards the exit. A Temple guard came running at them from out of the tunnel, but Pry took him out with a shot to the head. Yaz looked around, but couldn't see Ryan anywhere. He'd been right beside them a second ago …

'Doctor? Where's Ryan?' She didn't reply. 'Doctor?'

'Tromos took him hostage.'

'What?'

Pulling off the leather vest, the Doctor glanced her way and grimaced. 'I'm a bit more hopeful than I was ten minutes ago. If I can talk him around, Ryan definitely can. I think he just wanted to get out.'

Yaz steered them towards the storm drain they'd come in through. 'This way.'

'Wait!' The Doctor helped her to rest Mariya against the wall before pelting down the corridor to one of the cells. She took a step back before delivering an almighty kick to the door. It flew open, she ducked inside and emerged a second later with her coat, tucking her sonic into the inside pocket. 'That's better. Ooh, I felt naked without this.'

Pry followed them into the tunnel, firing off a few final rounds at the Temple guards in the arena. Fraught, he ran to Mariya's aid. 'Mariya! What happened to her?'

'It's not their fault,' Mariya muttered, sweat running down her face. 'He was behind me. I wasn't looking.'

'Pry …' Yaz said as gently as she could. 'We *have* to get out of here.'

Pry nodded. He went down the ladder first and waited at the bottom. Between the two of them, they lowered

Mariya into his arms. The Doctor went down behind her, and Yaz pulled the grate back over her head.

'Can you walk?' Pry asked his wife.

'I'll try ...' She didn't look at all good. Her lips were chalky white and her skin clammy.

'Let's get as far away from here as possible,' the Doctor said, sealing the manhole shut with her sonic. 'They'll be bound to follow us and that won't hold them long.' She once again supported Mariya, and Yaz led the way.

It was slow going with Mariya barely able to walk, but they descended deeper and deeper into the sewers below Kanda City, before Yaz found the service panel that connected the drainage system to the network of sea caves.

'I ... I need to rest,' Mariya whispered.

Pry and the Doctor laid her down. 'Yaz, get her some water.'

Yaz did as instructed. There was something reassuring about the cold silence of the caves. Yaz listened for the trickle of water and found an underground pond, sort of like a rock pool. She guessed either rainwater had trickled down, or it came from a natural spring from below. As Yaz crouched to fill her water canister, she heard footfall. Startled, she pressed herself behind rocks, fearing guards.

'Mother!' It was only Jaya and Tempika catching them up. Jaya fell at her mother's side. 'What happened.'

'Temple scum,' Pry growled.

Tempika helped Yaz. 'Here, you need to purify that.' He gave her one of the tablets they all seemed to use. Yaz added it into the bottle and gave it a shake.

When they returned to Mariya, she was looking even worse. Yaz held the water bottle to her lips, but she could hardly lift her head.

'Mariya? Mariya, my love, you hold on.' Pry cradled her in his arms.

'Pry ... Jaya. You ... you look after him.'

And that was when Yaz knew Mariya wasn't going to make it. She'd seen this before. Sometimes, it's like you could see life leaking away. She was beyond help.

'Mother ...?'

'No!' Pry said. 'You're going to be fine. You're fine.'

Mariya's breathing came in sickly, shallow rasps.

The Doctor took Yaz by the hand and led her away. 'Let's give them a moment,' she whispered. The Doctor had seen it too.

Yaz backed away. Mariya went limp in Pry's arms. Jaya buried her head in her hands and Tempika put an arm around her shoulders.

By the rock pool, the Doctor pulled Yaz into a hug. 'Hello.'

'Hey,' Yaz said sadly. She inhaled the Doctor's smell, although every time they hugged, her friend smelled different: sometimes like solder or engine oil, sometimes like peppermint or beeswax or Earl Grey tea.

'Did you know her well?'

'Not really. But she was good. They saved my life.'

The Doctor patted her arms. 'We're going to help them. Now that I'm free, we can get to work. Starting with this ...' Reaching into her coat pocket, the Doctor took out her sonic screwdriver and pointed it at the rock pool. She scanned the water.

'What's that for?'

'Testing a theory.'

'And?'

The Doctor checked the results. She made a triumphant 'hmph' noise. 'I was right. Usually am.'

Behind them, Pry howled. It was the worst, saddest noise Yaz had ever heard; so full of pain it cut all the way through her. Pry stood and punched the side of the cave so hard a chunk of rock crumbled. 'This!' he roared. 'This ends now.' He marched away into the dark of the caves.

Yaz went to run after him.

'Let him go,' the Doctor said, catching her at the elbow. 'He's allowed to be angry.'

'You don't know him like I do. He was dangerous *before* he was angry.'

The Doctor nodded. She knelt next to Mariya's body and stroked hair off her face. 'I'm so sorry,' she told Jaya. 'I'm the Doctor.'

'The Good Doctor?' Jaya looked up at her through her tears.

'The Doctor Who Tries To Be Good? Doesn't have quite the same ring to it, does it?'

'Where did Pry go?' Yaz asked as gently as she could. There *was* another training day on how to break bad news to family members, but it was typical how it had all gone out of her head right now when she actually needed the skills.

'I don't know,' Jaya sobbed. 'You know my father. He'll be looking for someone to blame.' Jaya sorted of folded into Tempika's arms and he held her close.

'I'm going to try to put things right,' the Doctor said quietly.

Yaz pulled the Doctor back. 'Doctor,' she said, low so that Jaya and Tempika wouldn't hear. 'This isn't our fault.'

'Isn't it?'

'No!' Yaz shook her head. 'We didn't tell them to start a bonkers religion based on a day trip we once made, did we? We didn't arm a whole bunch of insurgents and monks!'

The Doctor sighed a deep sigh and perched on a damp boulder. Some natural light filtered down through the rocks and everything glowed a beautiful blueish-silver. 'Oh Yasmin, you are as kind of heart as you are tiny of hand.'

Yaz couldn't not laugh. 'Thanks! I think.'

'I sometimes think I should superglue a rear view mirror on top of the TARDIS. I spend so much time running forwards, I sometimes forget to look back.' Yazmin sat right next her, their thighs pressed together. The Doctor went on. 'My people, the Time Lords, had a Book of Truths of their very own and the first rule was that we're not meant to get involved. We're supposed to be silent little ghosties, never leaving any footprints.'

Yaz gave her knee a nudge.

'And you know what? I pretty much tore up the rulebook when I was your age.'

Yaz smiled. 'Why doesn't that surprise me?'

'But I forget sometimes. These things we do … it all means something after we've gone. Legacy. Sounds very grand, doesn't it? Maybe sometimes I should stick to good old campsite rules: leave it as you found it.'

It was odd to see her like this. 'Doctor, you totally *should* look back – to see how much *good* you've done. You make stuff better. You do! If we've ever … made changes … they've always been from a place of good. If I've learned one thing this year it's that sometimes in the cosmos there is fundamental good and bad. And I always, *always* know you're on the side of good.'

The Doctor smiled. 'Ooh, you're a wonder at the pep talk, you are, Yasmin Khan. And you're usually right too. We've made a mess. Accidentally, but we have. Good news is, when you make a mess, you say sorry and get out the wet wipes. We can make this right.'

She sprang up and darted back to where Tempika had now covered Mariya with his robes. 'Jaya. I'm sorry to bother you, but did your father say where he was going?'

She wiped her eyes. 'No. But I'm guessing he's heading back to the rebel base in the West Cliffs.'

'That's what I'm worried about,' Yaz said.

'Come on,' the Doctor said. 'Let's carry your mother home. She deserves a proper farewell when the time comes.'

Jaya thanked her and, saying nothing, Tempika kissed the top of Jaya's head.

'You two are a bit cute aren't you?' The Doctor said, handing Jaya a spotty handkerchief from inside her coat. 'It's clean. Probably. I'm so, so, so sorry about your mum.'

Jaya looked up at her. 'I … thank you.'

'Listen … this world … Lobos … this world is for you two. I mean it. This won't be in vain, I promise.'

'Who are you?' Jaya's eyes glistened.

'Oh I'm just a fan, passing through.'

'A fan?'

'I'm such a fan of *you*. Such a fan of love.'

Tempika took Jaya's hand in his.

'I'll tell you what I'm not a fan of ...' the Doctor said, that steely look back in her eye, '... hate.'

Chapter 20

Back at the Temple, one of the monks carefully placed a plaster on Graham's head. He'd fallen during the stampede from the stadium and had a nasty gash just about his left eye.

'Your Grace,' said the medic to Mykados, 'please allow me to examine you.'

'I'm perfectly fine!' Mykados snapped, although Graham noticed he was walking with a definite limp since they'd both taken that tumble.

'Is that better?' asked the young monk.

Graham reached up and felt his head. 'Yeah, that's great, thanks mate.' The young monk excused himself as Father Ornid entered the little medical bay they were presently in. It was a small ward with six beds symmetrically set out on either side of the room. It smelled of alcohol and antiseptic.

There was another tremor from below and some of the jars of potions and lotions rattled on the shelves.

Ornid steadied himself against the doorframe, but Mykados swooped on him like a vulture. 'Report. What's going on out there?'

Ornid was tight lipped. 'Mayor Belen is calling for an urgent meeting. He took his young daughter to the arena and he's not happy. Not happy at all.'

Outside the medical room, Graham heard voices, doors slamming, heavy footfalls. ''Ere, what's going on? What's really going on?'

'High Priest Mykados.' Ornid pulled himself tall. 'Some people are saying the Good Doctor is furious with us. That this is our punishment for the way we've treated the newcomers.' He pointed at Graham. 'Some of the families are packing their bags and fleeing Old Town – heading down the coast or into the hills.'

'This is madness! Hysteria!' Mykados hissed.

'Is it? The Eyes can't locate the rebels, or the woman and Rasmin, and that monster Tromos is still on the loose! This is chaos! The very ground beneath our feet is alive! They're saying …'

'They're saying what, Father Ornid? Spit it out!'

Ornid looked deathly pale. 'That this is the day foretold in the Book of Truths.'

Mykados rounded on Graham, gripping his chin in his bony fingers. 'Is that what you are? An omen of the apocalypse?'

Graham shook his head. 'No, mate. Retired bus driver.'

Mykados relaxed his grip. 'I always wondered what the end would look like when it finally came. But I never imagined it would look so … mundane. But I suppose that's how the wolves get through the door. Sheep's clothing.'

'It's not the end, Mykados,' Graham said nervously. The Doctor and his Grace were always so much better at the big rousing speeches. 'Every end is a new start if you want it to be.'

'Indeed. So it is written,' Mykados said, now staring out of the window, looking down on Old Town. 'The sun will set on our earthly era and a new dawn of the spirit will reign in eternity.'

'What's that supposed to mean?' Graham asked. He was starting to regret sneaking out of those Sunday School lessons to go fishing when he was a lad.

The earth shook again, this time more severely. Some bottles slid off the shelves, shattering on the hard floor.

'I must pray on this!' Mykados announced, his robes twirling. 'I will be in the Great Chapel.' He looked to the guard on the door. 'Keep him in here for now.'

As Mykados and Ornid swept out, Graham wondered if it was time to read this Book of Truths and see if there was even a scrap of truth in it. More to the point, if it offered any fine detail on what happened, allegedly, when the end was finally to come.

Ryan's eyes flickered open and the most beautiful pink-orange sunset blinded him. Little black birds darted across the sky. He could be lying on a beach right now. Somewhere hot on a sun lounger, before his gran … before the Doctor.

The Doctor.

He sat up straight, ready to run or fight. He was dizzy. He remembered he couldn't breathe … Tromos had squeezed so tight, too tight, and it had all gone black.

Ryan blinked. He was on tiles. Dusty, cracked tiles. As his vision swam into focus, he saw he was in a shopping centre. A derelict shopping centre. He was sat in what had probably been a fountain at one point, long since dried out.

All the glass in the ceiling was smashed and birds flew in and out of the skeleton of the mall. Shop signs dangled from cables, and bits of mannequin bodies were strewn up and down the old escalators. 'Whaaaaat?' He rubbed his head.

'Hurts …' said a deep, rough growl.

Tromos.

Ryan sprang to his feet and looked around for his captor. He couldn't see him. 'Tromos?'

'It hurts.'

Cautiously, Ryan clambered out of the fountain. He followed Tromos's voice and saw the huge, shaggy loba cowering underneath an old hot dog stall. Was he trying to be funny or something? 'You OK, bud?'

Tromos tugged at the collar around his neck. A red light flashed on and off. 'Please … stop this … the pain.'

'You could have killed me!'

Tromos looked up at him with watery eyes. 'What are you?'

'Huh?'

'Monk?'

'No.'

'Rebel?'

'Also no.'

'Then what?'

Ryan held his hands apart. 'I dunno, bruv. Just, like, travelling or whatever.'

Tromos continued to pull on the collar. 'Get it off!' He curled his fists into balls and punched them into the tiles, splitting them apart.

'Stop!' Ryan dared to take a couple of steps closer. 'You're gonna hurt yourself.'

'Help me …' It was a such a tiny whisper from such a big thing.

'Hold up. If I get that thing off, how do I know you're not gonna rip my head off?' There was a gammy, red wound on his shoulder, but it didn't seem to be giving him too much grief.

Tromos narrowed his eyes. 'You have my word.'

'Got anything a bit more substantial?'

'My word has honour.' Tromos jabbed his bare chest with a claw. 'I am the last of the loba soldiers. I fought for Lobos.'

Ryan remembered Gran telling him the fable of the Lion and the Mouse when he was little. How did it go? The lion is gonna eat the mouse, but the mouse tells the lion that eating him will bring no honour. The lion lets the mouse go, but is then captured by hunters. Remembering the lion's kindness, the mouse chews through the nets and sets the lion free.

Ryan wasn't sure if he was the mouse or the lion in this situation. More importantly, he couldn't remember how the story ended. Did the lion then eat the mouse? Or kill the hunters?

'If I try and help you, will you help me? I need to find my mates. I need to save my Gr … aham.' Ryan figured having a friend like Tromos probably wouldn't hurt his odds. But the hulk's pupils were pinpricks, and he was still drooling. It could be that he'd been pumped full of drugs, but Ryan had no way of knowing that.

'You have my word ...'

'Ryan.'

'I would be in your debt.'

Ryan paced the mall floor. 'Oh I must be out of my tree ...' He knelt down alongside Tromos. 'Let me get a look, yeah?'

Tromos bared his neck to Ryan.

'Any sudden moves, and you're on your own, yeah?'

Tromos growled his approval and Ryan examined the collar. It was sealed shut at the back, some sort of woven chains, a bit like a bike lock. As he touched it, he recoiled. It was emitting short, sharp electric shocks. 'Ow!'

'Hurts ...'

'Yeah, I bet.' Ryan sighed and rose to his feet. 'Well we're in a shopping centre I guess. Wait here. We're gonna need some really, really big bolt cutters. And you need a bandage for that shoulder too.'

Tromos looked up at him. Ryan looked into his eyes, ignoring everything else but his expression. 'Thank you,' Tromos muttered. 'You are ...'

'I am what?'

'First human to show Tromos kindness.'

Ryan gulped back a whole bunch of feels. 'Yeah. Well. Just call me the Mouse.'

Chapter 21

Taking it in turns, the Doctor, Yaz, Jaya and Tempika silently and respectfully carried Mariya's body through the network of tunnels and caves. Tempika regularly used a tracking device which, he explained to Yaz, led him back to the rebels so he could quickly relay information to Jaya.

As they arrived back in the main rebel encampment, some others ran to their aid. 'What happened?' Dayna asked. 'I'm so sorry ... I came straight back here when everything fell apart at the arena.'

'It's Mother,' Jaya said mournfully.

'Mariya! No!' said one of the human rebels, hand over his mouth.

They carefully placed the body on one of the camp cots. Word spread and soon a crowd gathered around. The rebels hugged one another and tried to comfort Jaya. It hurt Yaz anew, a keen ache under her ribs. Mariya was so loved here. She'd be so sorely missed.

The Doctor slipped out of the huddle and pulled Dayna to one side. 'Where's Pry?'

'I don't know.' The loba shook her head. 'He stormed in without saying a word and took off after the excavation team.'

'Second question: Tromos grabbed our friend. Can you trace his collar?'

She shook her head. 'I lost the signal back at the arena. Wherever he is, the collar's malfunctioning.'

'OK, never mind. Thank you.'

'Doctor,' said Yaz, guiding her away from the mourners. 'The excavation team are mining underneath the hillside in Old Town. Pry's planning to topple the Temple. Literally.'

'Well that's a terrible idea.'

'You think?' Yaz said sarcastically.

Tempika completed a tour of the site. He looked flustered and spoke with urgency. 'Doctor, Yaz, I can't find the stockpile of explosives. Pry … Pry must have taken them. We don't have much firepower left but …'

'But enough?' said Yaz.

He shook his head. 'I honestly don't know.'

Yaz guessed Pry thought it was time to speed the schedule along a little.

The Doctor took off down the widest of the tunnels. 'This way?'

'Doctor!' Yaz ran after her. 'Shouldn't we … I don't know … make a plan or something?'

'This is the plan! We run down this tunnel towards the grief-stricken, rebel leader and make him see the error of his ways! Easy!'

Yaz grabbed the Doctor's arm. 'Pry is dangerous. More dangerous than ever, now.'

'No.' The Doctor pointed out of the tunnel towards Jaya. 'That's not true. He needs a timely reminder, that's all.'

The ground started to quake.

'It's OK,' Yaz said. 'It does this sometimes.'

But this time it didn't stop. Soot and dust started to sprinkle down. The whole cavern seemed to rear up and jolt, so violently that Yaz was swept of her feet. She and the Doctor collapsed into each other in a heap.

'I'm not sure it's *very* OK, Yaz.'

'You might be onto something,' said Yaz uncertainly. This was a bad one.

The Doctor gripped the cave wall and clawed her way back into the main cavern. 'Everybody take shelter!'

Overhead a huge stalactite came free and crashed down. The rebels scattered, screaming. Tempika dragged Jaya towards the tunnel.

'Wait!' Jaya screamed. 'What about Mother!'

'We'll come back for her! We have to go, Jaya!'

'Run!' the Doctor shouted over the deep, hungry rumble of the earth. 'This whole chamber is going to collapse! Out! Out! Out now!'

The rebels grabbed what they could, but there was no time. The scaffolding supposed to support the walls buckled, metal girders bending and breaking as the walls caved in. Huge boulders crashed down and thick dust filled the air.

'Doctor!' Yaz said. 'The TARDIS ...'

'Too late. We'll be killed. Come on!'

Covering her mouth and nose with her sleeve, Yaz ran after the Doctor. She looked over her shoulder and all she saw was a hint of blue paint through the rubble. The TARDIS was buried.

Alone, Mykados stood before the window in the Great Chapel. All around him candle flames flickered and bobbed in the evening breeze. Mykados looked up at the benevolent face of the stained-glass Good Doctor. It was tainted now by the face of the interloper in the medical bay.

How?

How could he look so like the Image but spit such vile venom?

Mykados's mind was filled with questions. Noise. Unwelcome noise. Impure questions and challenges to his ironclad faith.

'O Good Doctor,' he said. 'At this time of discord, I pray for guidance.'

He fell to his knees at the altar.

'Why, O Good Doctor? I know you have a master plan for Lobos and everything that happens is part of your glorious destiny, but what possible role could these intruders play in your great scheme?' He shook his head. 'Are their brazen lies designed to test my faith? False prophets, offering easy answers. I know the road to Tordos is littered with temptation and I fear those of feeble heart will listen to their lies.'

The ground shook, trembled lightly, and Mykados gripped the altar. It seemed to pass.

'Everything you have ever taught me, they deny. I know every word of the Book of Truths, and they dare to tread in your holy house and question them. The word of the

Good Doctor is the foundation of Lobos. Humankind were made in your image. Loba are our slaves. It is the way. It is the right way.' He felt his resolve harden. 'They must be executed. All of them. The people of Lobos – human and loba – must see what happens to those who challenge the word of the Good Doctor!'

The ground shook violently, like a sudden shockwave rippling through the mountain. Mykados was catapulted backwards down the gentle stairs that led to the altar. Overhead, the mighty chandeliers swung wildly from side to side.

There was a tell-tale crack. Mykados rolled over and saw a hairline fracture spread across the Good Doctor's face in the window. Then another, like a spider's web in the glass.

'No!' Mykados cried.

But his scream was drowned out by the shattering glass. As the earth shook, the high walls contorted and the entire window exploded inwards. All Mykados could do was shelter his face with his arms.

The quake subsided.

Mykados saw his hands were covered in cuts. He felt his face: he had one on his forehead too. He looked up and all that was left of the Good Doctor were a few jagged shards.

'My lord …' he muttered. He felt hot tears roll down his cheeks. He felt it: the holy presence. In that moment, the Good Doctor had truly been at his side. 'You sent me a sign. It is *time*.'

Chapter 22

Graham picked himself up off the floor of the medical bay. 'You all right?' he asked the guard, who had seemed to hit his head on the medicine cabinet as he went down.

He rubbed the back of his head. 'Um, yes, I think so.'

'Did you hear that?' Graham asked. 'That big smash? What was that?' It had sounded huge, like an explosion of some sort.

'Guards!' A call came from outside. 'Guards!'

The young man seemed flustered, unsure of what to do. 'Um … wait here,' he told Graham and went to investigate the commotion.

Graham counted backwards from ten before trying the door handle. It wasn't locked. Opening it a couple of inches, he peeped out and saw a cluster of guards and monks in disarray. They seemed to be pointing downstairs, towards the main chapel. That smash … It could be that big ugly window with my mug on it, he thought. It was certainly loud enough.

It was now or never. He slipped through the gap and stuck to the walls, trying to be as ninja-like as possible. As the guards raced downstairs, Graham prowled upstairs towards Mykados's reading room, and in search of answers.

Ryan gritted his teeth and slid the bolt cutters around Tromos's collar. 'Right, mate. Hold *very* still.' It looked like it was sealed by a fairly basic chain, but it *could* be booby-trapped.

'Just do it,' Tromos growled, knelt before him.

Ryan squeezed the cutters together and pressed down hard. It was solid. 'Sorry …' he wheezed as he applied all the pressure he could. The collar popped open and clattered to the floor in front of Tromos. Ryan took a big step back, anticipating it might explode.

But nothing happened. The red light continued to flash on and off.

Tromos stood, pulling himself up to his full height and towering over Ryan. He *must* be over seven foot tall, Ryan thought. 'Is, um, that better?'

'Yes.'

'Good. Good.'

'Thank you.'

'It was nothing.'

Tromos looked down at his massive paws. They trembled slightly. 'Pills,' he said.

'What?'

'I need pills. For pain.'

'OK.' Ryan nodded. 'Come here, though. Let me patch up that shoulder.' What had they done to this poor guy? As Tromos knelt before him again, his swollen body reminded

Ryan of the lads down the gym in Sheffield who were clearly taking stuff to bulk them out – muscles on muscles on muscles. What had they pumped Tromos full of?

'Well where are they?' He pressed some gauze on the wound and Tromos flinched.

'Prison.'

'OK.' It seemed like Tromos wasn't going to hurt him, but he did wonder if these pills also kept him calm. Hopefully he wouldn't need to find out. 'I need to find my mates. I don't even know if they got out of the arena in one piece.'

Tromos seemed to sniff the air. 'The arena. It no longer burns.'

'Good, I guess.'

'I will help you. I owe you my freedom.'

'Nah, you don't owe me that. But thank you.' Ryan finished taping down the dressing. 'There! That should do it.'

Saying no more, Tromos rose and skulked through the debris of the mall, towards one of the exits. Ryan had to jog to match his stride. 'Be quick,' the hulk said. 'Need pills. Without pills, I will kill.'

Well, that answered that then.

They were lost.

No one was *admitting* they were lost, but Yaz strongly felt they were going around in circles. Some of the tunnels had collapsed in on themselves during the big quake and they had to double back on themselves to find alternative routes.

'I can track Pry,' Tempika said, fiddling with his tracking device. 'There's a tracker on the excavator.'

'No!' the Doctor said with her strange authority. It was funny, thought Yaz, that she never really *asked* for people to follow her, yet everyone always seemed to end up devolving responsibility to her. 'Right now, the priority is to get out of these tunnels. As Pry mines deeper into the mountainside, the more precarious the caves seem to get. There's a saying where I come from: "No one enjoys being buried alive."'

'Yeah we have that saying here too,' Jaya said drily.

'Ha! I like you!' Although the resistance had gone in different directions, nine of them had followed Jaya and the Doctor this way. Now they all looked to the Doctor. She licked a finger and held it up to the air. 'This way! We keep going up and eventually we'll reach the surface.'

Jaya shook her head. 'I have to find my father.'

'We will,' the Doctor said earnestly. 'But, if push comes to shove, he could dig himself out in his little digger. These people can't. We help them to safety first.'

Jaya conceded with a nod.

They walked on, helping each other climb over rock falls. It was tiring, physical stuff and Yaz's body was now reminding her, painfully, that she hadn't slept or eaten properly in almost two days *and* her knee was bandaged. 'Doctor?' she whispered. 'What if Pry was buried? The excavator could have been damaged.'

The Doctor took her hand and helped her over some boulders. 'Something very ugly in me would be tempted to say he, quite literally, brought it on himself. But no.

Tempika seems to think his digger is still digging. And I need Pry alive. He's vital. Mostly because I need to knock his and Mykados's heads together at some point if there's ever going to be peace on Lobos again.'

The Doctor held an arm out and Yaz crashed into it. 'What?'

'Look. Up ahead.'

Yaz squinted and saw a torchlight bobbing towards them. She spun around and motioned at Jaya and Tempika behind her. 'There's someone coming, take cover!'

She pressed herself into a nook. If the Temple guards found them now, she suspected they'd shoot to kill. There was a familiar whirring noise. Yaz dared to look out and saw an Eye drifting towards them. The Temple had sent Eyes into the mines to flush them out.

'Freeze,' the Doctor whispered. 'With any luck it has motion, not body heat, sensors.'

'Tempika …?' a crackling voice said through the hovering device. 'Brother Tempika? Are you there?'

Tempika crawled out from behind some rocks. 'I'm here!'

'Tempika!' Yaz said. 'Way to be stealthy!'

'It's OK!' Tempika smiled. 'It's one of ours. It's Sister Lalla from Old Town orphanage. She's on our side.'

'Ah, I suspected as much.' The Doctor confidently stepped out from her hiding place. 'Pleasure to meet you, Sister Lalla.' She shook the air in front of the Eye as if it had a hand.

'You're the blasphemer …' the voice said.

'That's me.'

'Sister, what's the matter?' Tempika said.

'Report to the Temple as fast as you can, my brother.'

'Why? What's wrong?'

Lalla replied but the line was bad and Yaz couldn't make out what she'd said. 'You're breaking up!' she said.

'I said, Mykados has … all of … faithful to the Temple at midnight … even women … letting women into the Temple!'

'He's letting women in the Temple?' Jaya said.

'Wow, things must be bad,' the Doctor added wryly.

'Did he say why?' Tempika asked.

'Negative. Just that anyone who bel … in the word of the Good Doctor must … to Midnight Mass.'

'Well this is a disaster!' Yaz said. 'All of Old Town in the Temple – and Pry is about to tunnel underneath it and blow it up!'

Even in the dim light of the torches, all the colour drained out of the Doctor's face. 'As above, so below. It'll be a massacre.'

Chapter 23

The Doctor froze, like there was something she needed to say, something on the tip of her tongue.

'What?' Yaz said.

'No. That *would* be a disaster, but it won't be because we're going to stop it.'

'How?'

'I forgot something really important: people aren't stupid. It was a mistake the Time Lords made, and why I never got on with them. Yaz! Sometimes it's easy to see why you might *think* people are following a herd, but they're not. The people of Old Town aren't sheep and they're not stupid.'

Oh Yaz just *loved* it when the Doctor went into metaphor mode. 'OK … and …?'

'We need to get to that Temple toot sweet, whatever that means.'

'It's French.'

'Ah, lovely, big fan of their Mr Kipling Fancies.' The Doctor stepped in front of the Eye. 'Sister Lalla, can you program a safe, clear route out of the mines for us?'

'Yes.'

'Good.' She turned back to Yaz. 'I need you to do a job. It might be dangerous.'

'Not a problem.'

'Take Tempika's tracking device and find Pry. Think you can talk him out of taking down a temple?'

'I like him. I think he likes me. I can try.'

'No,' Jaya interjected. 'He's my father. I should go.'

'Any other day, I'd agree, but I need you,' the Doctor said.

'Me?'

'You *and* Tempika. You as well, Dayna. I'll explain everything, I promise, but we have got to get to that Temple while there's still a Temple to get to.'

Jaya didn't look convinced, but she nodded.

'Here,' said Tempika, handing Yaz his tracking device. 'It just counts down how many metres away you are from the excavator.'

Yaz examined the display. It looked pretty self-explanatory.

'Be safe,' the Doctor told her. 'If you think the tunnels aren't safe any more then …'

'Run.'

'Run for your life. Or run for the TARDIS and dig her out. Get inside and you should be safe if there's a cave-in.' The Doctor took out her sonic and activated it until it made a reassuring beep. 'There. Linked up. I'll be able to find the TARDIS no matter what.'

Yaz nodded. 'I can do this.'

'Yeah, you can.' The Doctor flashed a brilliant grin and then took off in the opposite direction. 'Come on team!

Can't be late for mass! Lead the way, floating creepy eye thing!'

Graham slipped into Mykados's reading room and winced as the door creaked. In the distance he could still hear shouting and hurried footsteps and everyone seemed to be heading in the direction of the chapel. With any luck, they wouldn't even notice he was gone.

Not wanting to draw attention to himself, he picked up a single glass lantern and carried it over to the bookcase. The Book of Truths, a huge, glitzy-gold, gem-studded affair, was held in its own special cabinet, which was unlocked. He lifted it out and slammed it onto the desk. 'Oof! Weighs a ton!'

He opened it up to the beginning. There was an illustration of the humans bowing before what could only be him. Ridiculous. The first chapter was called *In the Time of the Savages*. '*In the beginning, Lobos was a savage planet of feral dogs known as loba*. Well that's a load of old tosh, ain't it? *The bloodthirsty natives ate their own infants, wed their own kin and killed without mercy. The first humans arrived on Lobos on a mission of kindness: to teach the loba the ways of civilised society.* Oh, for crying out loud! Who buys this garbage, honestly?'

Graham remembered the last time he was in this office: there was that locked cabinet. He left his place at the desk and carried the candle over to the tall, slim cupboard in the corner. Sure enough there was still an ornate padlock, sealing it shut. 'Hmm. Wonder what secrets Mykados has locked up in here?' he mumbled to himself.

He gripped the lock and gave it a waggle. It was a fairly sturdy affair, and he doubted Mykados just left a key lying around. Still, he ducked over to the desk and tried the drawers, which were also locked. Desperate times called for desperate measures. On the desk was the bronze bust of his head. Graham grasped it under the chin and tried to lift it. Heavy, but not too heavy.

'Here we go, then ...'

He heaved it up, lifted it over his head and slammed it against the lock. It chipped the wood finish but the lock didn't budge. With a grunt of effort he smashed it against the lock again and again until the whole lock cracked and clattered to the floor. Exhausted, Graham let the bust fall, where it rolled into the corner.

He wiped his brow with his sleeve and prised open the cabinet. Inside he saw shelves piled with papers, journals and folders. On the middle shelf was an important-looking, leather-bound journal, bursting at the seams with bits of parchment. 'Right then, what have we got in here?'

Ryan and Tromos had stolen a vehicle that had been abandoned outside the arena during the stampede. Ryan wouldn't ever brag about it, but of course he knew how to hot-wire a car – he was a mechanic. And it turned out prison buggies on Lobos were a lot like cars on Earth. Ryan drove because Tromos, it was clear, was in no fit state to.

The gargantuan loba looked almost comical hunched up beside Ryan in the front seat as they zipped through the narrow streets of Old Town. They must have looked like they were in *Mario Kart*.

Something was up, though. The townsfolk were leaving their houses and caravans in droves, some in their nightwear, and walking uphill towards the Temple. 'What's going on?' he asked Tromos, who ignored him.

Swaddled in some monk's robes to shield his face, Tromos seemed to be biting down on his teeth. He wasn't blinking, just staring ahead blankly.

'OK,' Ryan went on. 'How you wanna play this, Tromos? How are you gonna break into a prison?'

'I am Tromos,' he snarled.

'Fair enough.'

But as Ryan steered the armoured buggy along the harbour side, he saw he needn't have worried. The front gates to the prison stood open, unguarded. Unchallenged, he drove the vehicle straight onto the concourse, bringing it to a halt by the main doors. 'Do you know where you're going?'

'Hospital.'

'OK. I'll come with you.' Weirdly, he felt safer with Tromos than he did without. And he still had his head attached, always a good sign.

Tromos barged into the grand front doors with a thick shoulder and they burst open with no resistance. The entrance hall was similarly deserted. 'Where are guards?'

It was funny, Ryan thought, that wherever they went in the cosmos, hospitals and prisons always looked pretty much the same. 'That's what I was thinking! Where is everyone?' There weren't even any Eyes patrolling. Ryan leaned over the front desk and saw there were rows of security monitors. Some screens were black, from the earlier raid Ryan guessed, but most still showed life in the cells. 'I got prisoners but no guards.'

'Listen,' Tromos barked.

Ryan strained. 'Church bells.'

Tromos strode off, smashing his way through another door. 'Hospital.'

'Got it.' Ryan followed him down a narrow corridor and then down spiral stone stairs towards the basement. Slit windows let salty sea air drift up and down the halls.

As they turned the corner at the bottom of the stairs, a monk leapt out at them, gun in hand. 'Freeze or I'll—'

Tromos grabbed him by the throat and lifted him clear off the ground.

'Tromos, no!' Ryan yelled. 'Put him down! He's just a kid!' He looked no more than fourteen or fifteen. 'I said put him down!'

Tromos's eyes blazed and the monk gasped and gurgled. His feet twitched in thin air.

'You're only a monster if you act like a monster, Tromos.'

Tromos let the monk collapse to the floor. Ryan kicked his weapon down the hallway. 'Just go,' Ryan told him, and the monk wisely fled. Tromos again stared at his claws as if they didn't belong to him, like he'd never seen them before.

'You're not a monster, Tromos. They did this to you.'

'I owe them pain.' Tromos continued towards the medical bay.

Ryan scurried alongside him. 'After we get these pills, will you come with me to the Temple? That's where the Doctor will be if something's going down, I know it. You can help us. Help us free all of Lobos.'

Tromos stopped and looked down at Ryan. 'Free?'

'Yeah. All loba. All humans. All free.'

There was a silence and then Tromos roared with laughter and resumed on his quest to the pharmacy. 'The loba will never be free while humans live.'

'That's not true,' Ryan shouted down the corridor. 'I've seen it before. You can all be free. You can. You're free now. I freed you and I'm human. But can you believe in me?'

Tromos stopped again and looked back at him. Ryan saw it in his eyes. Tromos *believed*.

All by herself, Yaz walked, crawled and climbed further and further, deeper and deeper into the hillside. She passed where the TARDIS was partially buried and, with every step, the distance between her and the excavator lessened. It was hard work, and some of the tunnels were so narrow she had to wriggle through.

The torch on the front of her helmet was starting to fade and soon she feared she'd have to navigate the tunnels in abject darkness. The thought alone made her feel claustrophobic. She knew air wasn't running out in the caves, but it didn't stop that thought from entering her head.

After she had walked for what felt like hours, the tunnels became wider, and smelled almost charred. The excavator, she thought, these tunnels are freshly dug.

With a renewed spring in her step, Yaz picked up the pace until she could hearing the whirring of the machine and smell its oily fumes. The beam from her helmet shone on the metal back of the excavator. Its engine was running, but it was stationary. 'Pry? Pry, are you there?'

She felt something cold and hard press into the back of her skull.

'Don't move, Yasmin.' It was Pry. He spoke gravely. 'You shouldn't have come down here.'

Yaz closed her eyes. 'Please, Pry. This isn't what—'

'What Mariya would have wanted? Wrong. We shared a vision. To destroy the Temple. And I won't let anyone stop me now.'

'Pry …'

'Even you. I'm sorry … I have no choice.'

Yaz held her breath and waited for the pain.

Chapter 24

The Temple of Tordos had never been this full. Bodies filled every space in the pews and the arches and the aisles: men, women, children and even loba servants. Mykados was unsettled at the presence of women and dogs in the Great Chapel, but these were extraordinary times, and they called for special measures.

Mykados, in his finest ceremonial robes, proceeded into the golden pulpit. The nervous chatter was a din and he held up his hand. 'Silence, my faithful children, all will be explained.' A hush fell over his enormous congregation. 'Thank you for coming to the Temple in the middle of the night.'

A gust of chill night wind blew in through the gaping hole in the window, blowing his thin hair into his face.

'Your Grace?' called Mother Capinella, the most senior of the Temple's women. Her wrinkled face peered out from her white hood. 'What is happening to Lobos? Are we safe?'

'Calm yourself, woman.' He looked out over the chapel. 'Tonight, in this very Temple, I received a visitation from the Good Doctor.'

The audience gasped.

'And not from the charlatans passing themselves off as celestial beings. No. I was blessed by the invisible spirit of the Good Doctor. I asked for a sign and He has answered.'

Once again, this revelation sent a ripple throughout the congregation.

'Silence! Please! We have much to do before dawn. As you all know, the Book of Truths is very clear. It is said, quite plainly, that the Good Doctor would return to Lobos once more at the planet's destruction. From there, those who followed His blessed teachings would be granted life eternal in the Kingdom of Tordos.'

None of this was news to the faithful. It was the first lesson one teaches children. If you are good, and behave in accordance to the Book of Truths, you will live forever.

'My children. Lobos has survived plague, and war, and terrorism. But now the earth itself is decaying. The ground on which we stand is rotten, crumbling under our feet.' Mykados took a breath. 'These are the last days of Lobos.'

Now there was a sharp intake of breath.

'Fear not! Fear not, my children. We have always known this day would come. If your faith is pure, your heart should not be afeared. We have always known that our true paradise lay far beyond this physical torment and in the land of Tordos. Children, together we will travel eternally in space and time!'

Mykados motioned to Brother Glezos, who carried forward the ceremonial wine in an ornate gold decanter. The church bells began to chime midnight. Doctor's Day had arrived.

'Yes, children. Tonight's mass will be our last. We will all imbibe the holy wine one final time.' He poured some wine into a ruby-stoned goblet. 'Faithful loba slaves are welcome to join us in the afterlife too. On this most holy day, we will bid farewell to Lobos once and for all. Doctor's Day is here and—'

'Is that my cue?' A voice cut across him. In the midst of the transept, one of the hooded brethren stepped forward from the others. With a magician's flourish, he whipped off his robes.

It was *her*. The blasphemer.

'Hi everyone!' she said. 'I think it's time for my bit.'

The cuffs dug into Yaz's wrists. Her arms were wrapped around the bar that ran across the front of the excavator cockpit. It bumped over the rough terrain, slowly and methodically chipping away the tunnel around them. 'Pry, stop,' she said.

'If you won't leave, there's no other choice,' he told her from the driver's seat. 'Don't say you weren't offered a way out.'

With a gun to her head, he'd tried to make her leave, but he'd underestimated just how stubborn she could be. To be honest, she'd never truly believed that Pry would shoot her in cold blood. 'This is mad, Pry. You don't need to do this.'

'This has gone on too long,' said Pry. 'Let's say I believed your tall tales of time travel … You just drop in and go again. I've lived on Lobos my whole life, a second-class citizen, a dog. The Temple is responsible for so much evil dressed up as good.'

'But come on! You're gonna blow yourself up! What about Jaya?'

'Her father will be a martyr.'

'Her father will be *dead*,' Yaz hissed. 'She already lost one parent today; don't let her be orphaned now. I know you're hurt. Mariya was … lovely, and brilliant, but she wanted you and Jaya together. You know it. She even *said* it!'

She saw doubt flicker in his eyes. 'No. This is our chance.'

'Pry, hundreds of people in Old Town will die if you detonate these explosives. How does that make you good in all this? Hundreds!'

'It's a just cause.'

The cuffs dug into her wrists. 'They're innocent, Pry! It's *never* just. Killing is never justified!' She was shouting now and didn't care.

Pry switched off the excavator engine and it ground to a halt. 'We're in position.'

'Pry …'

'Last chance. I let you go now and you run fast enough, you might just be clear of the mines when I blow.'

'No. If you're here, I'm here.'

'As you wish. Fool.'

A voice drifted down the black tunnel. 'I think it's time for my bit.'

'Doctor?' Yaz said, twisting round to look behind her.

Pry jumped down from the cockpit. 'Show yourself!'

Instead of the Doctor, a glow floated down the corridor towards them: an Eye. It was crackly but it was relaying the Doctor's voice, wherever she was.

'What's this?' Pry growled.

'It's the Doctor.' A smile broke out on Yaz's face.

'Kill her!' Mykados pointed a trembling finger at the Doctor.

'Oh, go on!' The Doctor marched to the centre of the altar. 'If you really wanna see a miracle, pull the trigger! I've got quite the party trick …'

But none of the guards or monks moved in for the kill. Instead, they hung back uncertainly.

'What are you waiting for?'

It seemed no guard wanted to be the one to open fire in the Temple.

'Ooh, Mykkie, you're losing your touch. Either that or the prospect of drinking poisoned wine doesn't have the appeal you thought it might.'

'Close your ears to her lies,' Mykados proclaimed.

'Why would I lie?' The Doctor spun on her heels and addressed the people of Old Town. 'I'm not sure we've been introduced. I'm the Doctor.'

The congregation looked to one another, confused.

'I know, I know. You were told a grumpy old man in a coat was going to come and save you. But that's not me. Oh, I've had a lot of faces, but there's always been me and there's always been the message.'

'What message is that?' Mykados sneered from his pulpit.

'Hope,' the Doctor said. 'Always hope. This is not the end, Lobos. The end of a chapter, perhaps, but the beginning of a new, better one.'

Now the congregation looked really confused.

'Don't be bewitched by this she-devil!' Mykados's eyes looked ready to pop out of his skull.

'Listen. Me and my friends did come here once before. I had the same message then, and I helped. That's what I do. When I left Lobos six hundred years ago, the human settlers and indigenous loba agreed to share power on the planet.'

This elicited a gasp. 'Lies!' a man towards the back heckled her.

'Mongrels,' an elderly woman sucked her teeth.

'It's true!' A new voice echoed around the chapel. Graham stumbled into the hall through one of the side chambers. He supported himself against the stone archway. 'Crikey there's a lot of stairs in this place.'

'See! That's Graham! Before we left last time, we posed for photographs, so it seems *some* people decided *his* face fitted and formulated your Good Doctor. But no, he's just my Best Graham.' The Doctor clapped. 'Where've you been? You're missing the big inspirational speech.'

Graham held a leather folder aloft, still struggling to breathe. 'I found these!'

'STOP HIM!' Mykados barked but, once more, the Temple guards looked baffled.

'Ooh, what have you got?' the Doctor said. 'Up you bob. Let him through.'

When the Doctor spoke, people listened. The congregation parted to let Graham make his way to the altar.

'I will not tolerate this!' Mykados sprayed saliva through the air. 'Guards, seize them!'

'Or ...' the Doctor said, holding up a finger. 'Who is keen to see what interesting factettes Graham has unearthed? I bet they're really juicy.'

'They didn't burn,' Graham panted.

'What's that?'

'The history books. They didn't burn. They kept them secret, hidden away.'

He gave the Doctor an old ledger and some partially burned documents. The Doctor scanned them in seconds. 'Oh well, would you look at that? People of Lobos: your Temple hasn't just been lying to you, they've been *wilfully* lying to you, and that rather changes things, doesn't it.'

'Silence!' Mykados now bolted down from the pulpit tripping over his robes and tumbling down the last steps.

'Never!' the Doctor shouted. 'All over Lobos, hear me now!'

In the mines, Yaz and Pry heard.

In the winding streets of Old Town, the Eyes were frozen, suspended in the air. Controlled by Dayna from a vessel disguised as a fishing boat in the harbour, every last one transmitted the strange woman's broadcast.

Men, women and children – human and loba – rose from their beds and came out of their homes to listen. The drunken sailors and fishermen listened. The patrons of the taverna listened.

Everyone listened.

Chapter 25

The Doctor held the manuscript aloft, keeping it out of the priest's reach. 'Ooh, Mykkie, you should have destroyed these centuries ago, but I suppose there is something irresistible about keeping secrets, isn't there. Lobos: I have in my hands an account of the peace treaty I helped to broker six hundred years ago. A treaty which signed into the law of this planet that power would be shared between humans and loba. At any given time, a member of both species would rule.'

Inside the church, the humans reacted angrily.

'Stop!' the Doctor said. 'If you are sitting here thinking you have some genetic superiority over the loba, you are sadly mistaken. Six hundred years ago, you were a sad, struggling colony. You humans only survived because of the hospitality of the loba. Anything else is a lie. Now you know the truth, what will you do with it?'

Outside, on the streets, the loba could scarcely contain their disbelief. The rumours ... the fairy stories ... could they really be true? The loba weren't born slaves?

Graham saw one of the monks step out of the pack. He lifted back his hood, and Graham saw it was Father Ornid. 'Mykados? Is this true?' That meant, thought Graham, that only the High Priest must have had access to the ancient documents; to the truth.

'Rubbish!' Mykados snapped. 'Ancient history! We all saw what happened when humans and loba mixed freely. A plague which almost wiped out the entire planet!'

'Well yes that would be convenient, wouldn't it?' The Doctor snatched the papers away from Mykados every time he went to pull them from her grasp. 'But here's a funny thing. I ran a little test on your untreated water supply. Contains a bacteria called F. tisseralos. Fairly harmless in small numbers, but occasionally a mutant strain causes some very, very serious poorly tummies.'

The audience look confused.

'You're saying they just had food poisoning?' Graham asked. 'Or water poisoning, anyway?'

'Pretty much. Sounds like it, albeit a very serious outbreak. It must have got into the water system. I tell you what it *wasn't* … a vengeful god striking you down. It was just a regular old illness.'

Mykados stepped forward and addressed the Temple. 'No! It was sin. The sinful mixing of human and loba brought about the plague!'

'Oh, what rot!' the Doctor said. 'If that was the case, how do you explain my chum, Jaya?'

The Doctor beckoned to her. She pulled off her robes and hurried onto the platform. A woman and a female half-human in the Temple. Big day for Lobos, Graham thought.

'Jaya? How are you?'

'I'm fine.'

'You're better than fine, you're perfect.' The Doctor cupped her pretty cheeks in her hands. She turned to the audience. 'Jaya has a human mother and loba father. She's engaged to be married to a monk.'

As the congregation expressed their consternation, Tempika ran to Jaya's side. 'Former monk,' he said. 'I want no part of this lie.'

'Listen!' the Doctor said. 'Actually, don't listen, *look*.'

Jaya took Tempika's hand.

The Temple finally fell silent.

'Just look. Look at all the harm they're not doing with their love.' The Doctor smiled. 'Look to the future. See the past, always see the past, but leave it where it belongs.'

Far below the surface, Yaz watched Pry watching the Eye. Although his back was to her, she saw him lift a paw to his face as if he was wiping away a tear.

'We could be there with them, you know?' Yaz said.

'But Mariya can't.'

Yaz shook her head and tried to go to him, forgetting she was tied to the excavator. 'That's not true. When my granddad died, my mum said I carried him with me in my heart. When we lose someone we love, we take them with us everywhere we go. We never forget them.'

Pry turned and looked at her.

'Mariya is with you, and she's with Jaya. She always will be.' Yaz nodded at the excavator. 'And you should be with Jaya.'

Pry looked from the Eye to the cases packed with explosives.

'I love you.' Tempika finally held his fiancée close to his chest for everyone to see. 'And I have nothing to be ashamed of.'

'There is so much life left to live on Lobos,' the Doctor.

'And what of the earthquakes?' Ornid asked.

'It's the rebels, not the Good Doctor!' The Doctor rolled her eyes. 'They've been quite literally undermining the Temple. Sabotage, plain and simple. *Not* an act of god.' She grasped the pitcher of wine from Brother Glezos and hurled it out of the window. 'I don't think we'll drink the Kool-Aid today, thanks.'

Graham turned back to Mykados and saw he had the goblet in his hands. He said softly, 'Mykados, mate, look, it's gonna be fine, yeah? Just put that down.'

It was as if the crowd was exhausted, too much information to process. Everything they knew was now called into question.

The silence was shattered as the main door to the chapel exploded in a flurry of splinters. The silhouette of Tromos filled the doorway, Ryan just behind him.

'Ryan!' said the Doctor cheerfully.

But Tromos wasn't feeling the cheer. 'You did this.' He pointed directly at Mykados. 'You did this to Tromos! So many years of pain.'

The huge loba charged forward down the middle aisle. Townsfolk screamed and leapt out of the way, falling on top of one another. Tromos roared. Spittle sprayed from his fangs.

'No!' the Doctor cried.

Tromos was going to tear Mykados to shreds.

Chapter 26

Tromos now galloped towards the altar.

'Doctor...?' Graham said, backing away.

'Say a little prayer, Graham,' the Doctor muttered. She sprinted across the altar to Mykados and seized him from behind, wrapping her arms around his chest.

'Get off me! What are you doing?'

'Saving you.'

The Doctor held up her sonic screwdriver and activated it. There was a shrill ringing and it glowed green. Tromos was just metres away. He pounced onto the altar. The Doctor screwed her eyes shut and ...

Graham heard a familiar grinding, whirring sound. A blue light flashed, and a cuboid shape took form around the Doctor and Mykados. As the light flashed it became more and more solid until only the TARDIS stood where they had been.

Tromos skidded to a halt in front of the blue box, his eyes wide.

Graham looked at the congregation. Their mouths hung open. They didn't even blink.

Ryan finally caught up with Tromos. 'What are you doing? Stop!' A couple of guards trained their guns on Tromos. 'He's cool,' Ryan told them. 'Are you cool?'

Tromos growled and curled his fists into balls.

'You gotta calm down or they are gonna kill you.'

Tromos roared in Ryan's face. His breath could have been better.

'You're free now. Don't mess it up.'

Tromos punched the sides of the TARDIS in frustration, but Ryan sensed he was cooling off. 'Calm.' He patted him on the back. 'Good man.'

One of the monks fell to his knees in front of the TARDIS. 'It's a miracle!' he proclaimed. 'The Good Doctor has returned!'

The door creaked open and the Doctor stepped out. 'It is absolutely, unequivocally *not* a miracle,' she said, pulling the monk to his feet. Mykados emerged from the TARDIS behind the Doctor, eyes wide with disbelief.

'Now listen up,' the Doctor went on. 'We'll get this straight once and for all – is someone writing this down? I am *not* a god. I am the Doctor and I just came to help. Got that? Get up off your knees! Now!' The guards and monks reluctantly did as they were told.

She marched up into the pulpit. Ryan and Graham followed.

'From this day forth, you are free to worship your gods in peace, but the loba are *free* and *equal*.' Her voice lowered, deadly serious. 'If you can't get on board with that, you'll *wish* I was the Good Doctor, because I'll return again, and there really *will* be a punishment.'

Some of the congregation went pale with fear.

The Doctor turned back to Graham and Ryan. She leaned in to whisper. 'Was that sufficiently scary? Do you think they'll do it?' she asked chirpily.

'Yeah,' Ryan said. 'I was bricking it.'

'Good-o. Was worried I'd laid it on a bit thick.'

They were interrupted by the sound of the goblet clanging to the marble floor. It rolled down the stairs, empty. Mykados held his throat.

'Mykkie!' The Doctor pelted down the stairs from the pulpit. 'What did you do that for?'

Mykados regarded the Doctor with pure, acid hatred in his eyes. 'I will not live in this world of yours.'

The Doctor's expression changed from pity to resignation. 'I suppose that's your choice. Because the world is changing, Mykados, for the better. Oh, if I know one thing, it's this: everything changes, *nothing* stays the same.'

Mykados choked and fell to his knees before his whole body turned stiff and he toppled to the side like a felled tree.

'No!' The Doctor knelt beside him and checked his pulse. She closed his eyelids, and her own, shaking her head. 'So needless.'

'Jaya!' A voice rang out, breaking the grave silence.

Graham saw a tall loba in a filthy jumpsuit standing where Tromos had torn the door off. And Yaz appeared at his side. Oh how his heart sang! She was safe. She needed an urgent bath, by the looks of it, but she was fine.

The pair ran down the aisle and the loba pulled Jaya into a tight embrace. 'Father, I love you.'

'I'm so sorry,' the loba muttered, and Graham wondered what he'd missed.

'Come here, you,' the Doctor said and gave Yaz a big hug. 'You did it! Knew you would.' She beckoned Graham and Ryan over too. 'Come on, group hug!'

Graham and Ryan got in on the action. 'Wait a minute, though, Doc. That bloody box has a remote control? Since when?'

The Doctor shrugged. '*If* my TARDIS worked properly, it'd do that every time. Been trying to fix that function for … well, since the beginning. Hardly ever works, but I figured out that we were standing pretty much directly on top of where it was buried. She was in range and I'd linked us up earlier, so I thought it was worth a shot. Can't believe it worked, to be honest.'

'What was Plan B?' Ryan asked.

The Doctor grinned. 'There wasn't one.' She gave the TARDIS a pat. 'But I had faith in the old girl. What have we learned today? Sometimes a bit of faith is enough.'

'Now,' Yaz said archly. 'Has anyone left anything behind this time?' She threw Ryan a pointed glance.

'We're not off yet,' said the Doctor. 'This time, we're not leaving *anything* open to interpretation.'

Chapter 27

At the top of the Temple was a great conference room with an imposing stone circle at its centre. The future of Lobos was gathered around the table, along with the Doctor and her friends.

'Mykados is dead,' the Doctor said gently. 'But there are a good many people responsible for the slavery of the loba. The Temple was complicit.'

Father Ornid represented the Temple. 'I shall launch an investigation into who knew the truth about the peace agreement.'

'That doesn't go far enough,' Pry said. Next to him sat a quiet Tromos. Three days after Doctor's Day, he was still suffering withdrawal – sweats and shakes – from all the chemicals they'd pumped him full of in the prison, but the Doctor had told him that he was going to be fine.

'It won't be easy,' the Doctor said. 'Some of those humans aren't going to want to give up their servants. They've been told their whole lives that this was the truth, they'll take some convincing.'

'We shall enforce it with all the power of the Temple,' said Ornid emphatically. 'This big blue box will become a symbol for peace, hope and unity, I promise.'

Bemus Belen spoke up finally. 'I, and the other mayors of Lobos, will continue to work alongside the Temple to usher in this new age. However, I'm also instigating an investigation to see if the Temple has been keeping any other secrets from my office.'

Ornid nodded. 'We will cooperate fully.'

'Well, I like the sound of that,' the Doctor said. 'If I have to leave a legacy, let it be that.'

Pry cleared his throat. 'I have already instructed my people to start reinforcing the old mine shaft. Hopefully the damage is reversible.'

'Who's going to be in charge? The Temple or the Mayor?' Yaz asked.

'What you need is someone to oversee both. I thought perhaps Tempika and Jaya,' the Doctor suggested. 'Tempika is from the Temple, Jaya is the daughter of the resistance. What perfect symmetry. What do you think? Up to the challenge?'

The young couple held hands on the table. 'Of course,' said Tempika. 'I can do anything with Jaya at my side.'

Jaya grinned. 'You are so sentimental sometimes. Yes, it's what my mother would have wanted.'

'It is,' Pry agreed.

A fleet of Eyes hovered at the edges of the room, seeing everything. 'There's only one thing left to do in that case,' the Doctor said. 'In the presence of all of Lobos, and recorded for posterity, will you sign into a law a ceasefire? A new peace treaty?'

On behalf of the indigenous loba, Pry signed first. Representing the human colonists, Father Ornid signed the parchment too.

The Doctor looked at Graham and the two shared a smile. 'And this time,' Graham said. 'When you tell it, tell the story right.'

Epilogue

Six hundred years later ...

Castele tucked Remini into his bed. 'Now lie back, my sweet child.'

'But how did the story end?'

She ruffled his fur. 'You know very well how it ends.'

'I like the way you tell it.'

Castele sighed at the familiar tug of war they performed every bedtime. It was a balmy night so she left the window open an inch or two. In the distance she could hear the surf shuddering over the pebbles in Graham Bay. She always found it so soothing. 'The Good Doctor landed the TARDIS on top of the Wicked Wizard and Lobos was free once more. King Tempika and Queen Jaya ruled for a hundred years, and thus began the Golden Age of Harmony.'

'And everyone lived happily ever after?'

'And everyone lived happily ever after!'

'What about the Doctor? What happened to her?'

'You know where the Doctor is!' Castele kissed him on the tip of his snout. 'Wherever there are people in trouble, wherever there's danger. Wherever there's cruelty or intolerance. Wherever there are mad kings and wicked tyrants, the Doctor and her friends will be there to help those who need her the most.'

She leaned over Remini and switched on his nightlight. Lights started to swirl around the room.

'Now that's enough. Go to sleep, little one.'

Remini lay back and watched the silhouette of a little blue box move across his ceiling amongst the stars.